A Precious Jewel

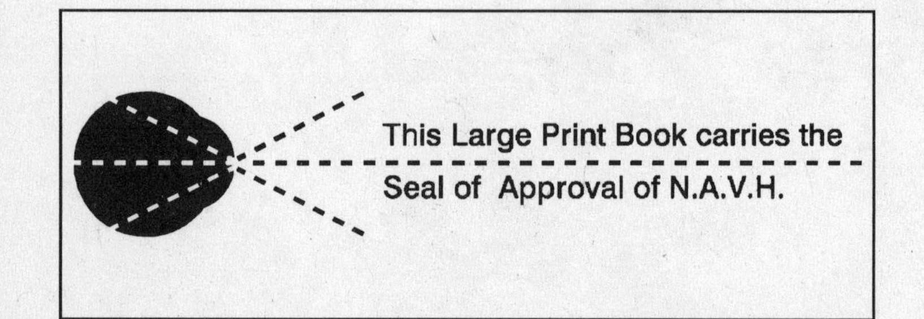
This Large Print Book carries the
Seal of Approval of N.A.V.H.

A Precious Jewel

Mary Balogh

THORNDIKE PRESS
A part of Gale, Cengage Learning

Detroit • New York • San Francisco • New Haven, Conn • Waterville, Maine • London

GALE
CENGAGE Learning™

Thorndike Press, a part of Gale, Cengage Learning.

Thorndike Press® Large Print Romance.
The text of this Large Print edition is unabridged.
Other aspects of the book may vary from the original edition.
Set in 16 pt. Plantin.

LIBRARY OF CONGRESS CATALOGING-IN-PUBLICATION DATA

Balogh, Mary.
A precious jewel / by Mary Balogh. — Large print ed.
p. cm. — (Thorndike Press large print romance)
ISBN-13: 978-1-4104-2610-9
ISBN-10: 1-4104-2610-6
1. Large type books. I. Title.
PR6052.A465P74 2010
823'.914—dc22 2010007004

Published in 2010 by arrangement with Dell Publishing, a division of Random House, Inc.

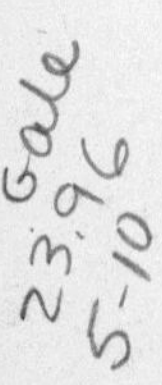

Printed in the United States of America
1 2 3 4 5 6 7 14 13 12 11 10

Dear Reader,

A Precious Jewel is that book of mine that insisted upon being written even though I knew it was quite impossible to write. Sir Gerald Stapleton was a minor character in *The Ideal Wife,* the hero's best friend, who several times bemoaned the loss of Priss, his longtime mistress, after she had left him to marry another man. I had no intention of writing his story, much less of writing Priscilla's. I was writing traditional Regencies at the time and could hardly have a working prostitute as a heroine and a beta male as a hero! When I tested the idea on a few fellow authors at a writers' convention, they agreed with me wholeheartedly.

But I was haunted by those two characters to such a degree that finally I had to write their story anyway. And I couldn't put it down once I had started. I completed it in two weeks! Then I put it up on a shelf to gather dust for a while, quite certain that my editor would have a fit of the vapors if she read it. At last I sent it in anyway and waited for it to be rejected. And waited. . . . When I finally called about it, I was told it was in copyediting. No rejection, no revisions!

That book became a great reader favorite in 1993, when it was first published. I hope you will still enjoy it today in this unaltered republication.

Mary Balogh

1

"I am afraid Sonia is indisposed today, Sir Gerald," Miss Katherine Blythe told the young man when he was shown into her private sitting room instead of being admitted to one of the downstairs salons, as usual. "She has taken a chill from walking in the park yesterday without adequate protection from the cold wind. I would scold her roundly if she were not feeling so miserable, poor girl."

"It was a chilly day yesterday," Sir Gerald Stapleton agreed. "I am sorry to hear that Sonia is not well, ma'am. Will you give her my regards? May I see her three days from now if she is recovered?"

Miss Blythe sat back in her chair and looked assessingly at the young man who stood before her. He was of average height, slim and well-formed, fashionably dressed. His face was pleasant even if not startlingly handsome. His fair hair curled into no particular style, but it was soft and clean. She appeared to come to a decision.

"I have one girl who is unexpectedly free for the next hour," she said. "Prissy has been with me for almost two months and is proving to be very satisfactory. Would you care to see her instead of Sonia for this evening, Sir Gerald?"

The young gentleman pursed his lips and considered for a moment. "I am afraid I am a creature of habit, ma'am," he said. "I have been seeing Sonia for three months."

"As you wish, sir," she said. "I am sure Sonia will be recovered in three days' time. I shall make the appointment for your usual time?"

He bowed. But he hesitated as he turned to leave. "Of course," he said, "I have no other plans for this evening."

Miss Blythe smiled at him. "Why don't you go down to the blue salon, Sir Gerald?" she said. "I shall send Prissy to you there and you may talk with her for a while. If you do not wish to stay after seeing her, you need not feel obliged to do so. If you do, well then, she is free."

He bowed again after nodding an assent, left the sitting room, and went downstairs to the blue salon, where a cheerful fire crackled in the hearth and took the chill from the March evening. He held his hands out to the blaze.

Perhaps it was time he tried someone new, he thought. He was indeed a creature of habit — he had told the truth in saying that. But he was also a man who feared commitment or obligation. He had avoided long-term relationships for all of his twenty-nine years and intended to do so for the rest of his life. Even his family relationships had never lasted long. Self-reliance was the only safe way to live, he had concluded long ago.

Yes, perhaps it was as well that Sonia was ill. Three months was quite long enough. Too long, perhaps. And when he thought carefully about the girl, he had to admit that there was nothing about her that he would miss.

He turned when the salon door opened. The young lady who stepped inside and closed the door quietly behind her seemed strangely out of place in Kit's house. She was small and dainty and dressed in a pretty green muslin dress, the neckline in a high frill beneath her chin, the sleeves puffed at the shoulders and then extending straight to the wrists. Her face beneath her short dark brown curls was pleasant and smiling, her gray eyes candid. She was pretty in a wholesome way. Her skin was creamy with a blush of color high on her cheekbones. She wore no cosmetics.

"Sir Gerald Stapleton?" she said. Her voice was light and musical, another discordant detail in the house. "I am sorry for your disappointment, sir, but Sonia really is dreadfully ill. Would you like me to entertain you for this evening?"

"Prissy?" he said, bowing to her. He did not usually think of bowing to any of Kit's girls. "It seems like a good idea, since I do not have any other plans for the evening."

She smiled, revealing to him white and even teeth. The smile extended all the way to her eyes, so that he was given the feeling that she really was pleased.

"I am glad," she said. "Will you come up to my room, sir? There is a fire there, too. It is a chilly evening, is it not?"

"Deuced depressing weather for March," he said, following her from the room and up the stairs, and wishing for some unfathomable reason that he had omitted the "deuced." The top of her head reached barely above his shoulders, he noticed.

"But how lovely to know that it is March," she said, "and that summer is to come. And how lovely it is to see all the spring flowers in bloom when one steps out of doors. Daffodils are my very favorites. We used to pick them by the armful when I was a girl."

She looked scarcely more than a girl now, he thought. She spoke in refined accents. But then all of Kit's girls did. She trained them to lose their regional accents and coarse vocabulary and to give the illusion of being ladies. Kit's house had a reputation for refinement.

The girl's room suited her, Sir Gerald thought when she opened the door and preceded him inside. It was decorated all in shades of blue. It was pretty and comfortable without in any way being either fussy or oversensuous. Plain mid-blue curtains were looped back from the bed, which was turned down neatly, ready for use, to reveal crisp white bedsheets and pillowcases.

She closed the door as quietly as she had the salon door earlier. She turned to him with a warm smile.

"How may I please you, sir?" she asked.

Her breasts looked small beneath the high bodice of her dress. So did her waist. Her hips looked as if they might be shapely enough, though it was difficult to know what exactly lay beneath the loose skirt of her dress, which fell from a fashionably high waistline.

"Would you like me to undress?" she asked.

"Yes," he said.

She turned her back on him, presenting him with the long line of buttons that extended from the neck of her dress to the hips. "Will you, please?" she said.

As he opened the buttons, he could see that she wore nothing beneath. She turned when he had completed his task, drew the dress off her shoulders and down her arms, let it fall to the floor, and stepped out of it.

Yes. Small breasts, but they were firm and uptilted. As he had suspected, her waist was small, her hips shapely. Her legs were slim, her stomach flat. There was none of the voluptuousness he normally expected of a whore. And none of the wiles, either — at least, not yet. She stood quietly for his inspection, her arms at her sides.

"Do you wish me to unclothe you, sir?" she asked.

He shook his head. "No." He shrugged out of his coat and raised his hands to his neckcloth. "Lie down on the bed."

She did so and lay quietly on her back there, watching him as he undressed. She did not cover herself.

"I don't like any tricks," he told her when he was almost ready to join her. "None of the little arts you girls know to make things proceed faster. I like to take it slowly at my own speed. All I want you to do is lie still."

Of course, none of them ever did. They seemed to feel that they were not doing their job if they did not use at least some of their considerable arsenal of arts until his control deserted him. Or perhaps it was in their own interests to make their encounters as brief as possible.

She smiled that warm smile again as he climbed onto the bed and on top of her, reaching up her arms for him, accommodating her body to fit comfortably around his, easing up her hips so that he could slide his hands beneath her.

"It shall be exactly as you wish, sir," she said. "I am here to give you pleasure."

He pushed himself inside her, and she raised her knees to hug his hips.

And she was as good as her word. Blessedly, during all the minutes that followed, she kept herself still, though she was relaxed and warm and yielding, very softly feminine. There were no tricks either with hands or hips or inner muscles. She allowed him to satisfy his appetite in the way he most liked to do it.

He sighed against her soft curls eventually and relaxed his full weight onto her. After a few minutes, when he was still hovering in the blissful state between waking and sleeping, he felt her lift one foot and reach down with one hand. A smooth sheet and warm blankets were drawn up about his shoulders. He sighed again and slept.

Fingers smoothing through his hair woke him. He did not know how long he had slept. He was warm and comfortable. Her hair smelled good. *She* smelled good and felt good beneath him.

"My time is up?" he said.

"Yes, sir," she said. "Almost."

When he turned to her after dressing, she was sitting on the edge of the bed, dressed in a modest pale blue dressing gown. She smiled at him.

"You are good, Prissy," he said. "There are not many . . . girls who are willing to do exactly as I ask."

"But it is my job and my pleasure to please you, sir," she said.

"I will be visiting you again," he said, one hand on the knob of the door.

"I shall look forward to it," she said.

He almost believed her as he let himself out of the room, so warm was her smile. She was a good actress as well as being very good at her profession.

He tapped on Kit's door.

"Ah," she said after summoning him inside. She set aside her book and removed the spectacles she was wearing. "You decided to stay, then, Sir Gerald? I thought you would once you had seen Prissy."

"I want her again," he said, "in three days' time. Is she much in demand?"

"Indeed she is," Miss Blythe said. "Almost all of her clients return and become regulars. You were fortunate that one of them was out of town this evening."

"Yes," he said. "Three days' time?"

She drew an appointment book toward her from a table at her elbow. "Four is the best I can do, I am afraid, Sir Gerald," she said. "Of course, Sonia will be free."

"Four days will do," he said. "The usual time?"

"I shall record it," she said. "I am glad that Prissy pleased you so well, Sir Gerald."

"Good night, ma'am," he said. He nodded to her and took his leave.

He did not, as he usually did when he left Kit's, go to White's in search of a card game and congenial company. He returned to his bachelor rooms and was in bed before midnight. He had a relaxed feeling of well-being and thought he would sleep well without the drugs of liquor and cards and male conversation until the early hours of the morning. He was not normally a good sleeper.

■ ■ ■ ■

Miss Katherine Blythe had eight girls working for her, all carefully chosen and well-trained — trained not only to provide the essential physical services, but also to do it in an atmosphere of some refinement. Her girls were young ladies who entertained gentlemen in order to earn a living. That fact was always the main focus of the very first lesson.

Not all gentlemen were allowed to visit. Miss Blythe had a personal interview with each of her girls every morning and listened to a report on the previous day's dealings. Any gentleman who was deemed unsuitable to the gentility of her establishment was denied further admittance. There were strict rules about what was allowed and what was not allowed in her house.

Each of her girls was allowed no more than three clients each day, and none was to stay for longer than one hour. A full half hour after each left was to be spent by each girl carefully cleansing herself. No gentleman ever acquired a disease from one of Miss Blythe's girls. And only rarely did one of her girls get with child. When it did happen, the girl concerned was roundly scolded for carelessness and then sent away and well looked after during her confinement. The child was found adoptive parents who would bring it up well.

Girls who had chosen prostitution as a profession coveted a place in Miss Blythe's finishing school, as she liked to call it. There was no more desirable place in London to work.

Priscilla Wentworth had been given one of those places with no trouble at all. And Miss Blythe had never made any secret of the fact that she was a favorite — *the* favorite.

"Sit down, dear," she said when Priscilla came for her morning interview the day after Sir Gerald Stapleton's visit. "Let me pour you some tea."

"Thank you, Miss Blythe." Priscilla crossed the room to take the cup and saucer from her employer's hand and seated herself on a chair beside the fire. "It is still chilly this morning, though the air is marvelously fresh."

"You went for an early walk as usual, then?" Miss Blythe asked. "I hope you dressed warmly, Priscilla, and that you did not go alone?"

Priscilla smiled. "After hearing your opinion of Sonia yesterday," she said, "I would not have dared to go out without my winter cloak. And I promised you after a scolding weeks ago that I would never again step outside alone."

"I would think not, too," Miss Blythe said. "You must always remember that you are a young lady, Priscilla."

The girl smiled.

Miss Blythe sighed. "But we will not pursue that thought today," she said. "You had three clients yesterday. Do you have any complaints?"

"No," Priscilla said. "None at all."

"You have no bruises?"

"No."

"No one spoke to you disrespectfully?"

"No."

"No profanities?"

"No."

"You have seen both Mr. Loft and Mr. Claremont several times before, of course," Miss Blythe said. "And I chose them with care at the start, Priscilla, as I choose all your clients. It struck me last evening when Sir Gerald Stapleton came for Sonia that he would be suitable for you too, dear. He seems a quiet and very proper young gentleman. I was glad when he came to make another appointment with you before he left. You must have pleased him. Did you like him?"

"Yes," Priscilla said. "I liked him very well."

"Sonia has never complained of him," Miss Blythe said. "He was not rough or demanding of too much, Priscilla?"

"No," the girl said. "I liked him. Will Sonia be annoyed with me?"

"For taking him away from her?" Miss Blythe said. "Sonia does not like regulars. She would prefer new challenges. But enough of that. Have you read the book I lent you?"

"I have not quite finished it," Priscilla said. "But I greatly admire the author's wit."

"Who is your favorite character?" Miss Blythe asked.

"Oh." Priscilla thought. "Mr. Darcy without a doubt, if one is to speak of heroes. I think him quite the most splendid hero of any book I have read. But Mr. Collins is a marvelous creation — a totally obsequious man without in any way becoming a caricature."

"Do you feel sorry for his wife?" Miss Blythe asked.

"Yes and no." Priscilla smiled. "She could have avoided marrying him, of course, so she had only herself to blame for all the tedium and embarrassment that followed. But then she married him to avoid the worse fate of being a spinster, and she made the best of it afterward and never complained. I think I admire her cheerfulness when she must have felt anything but cheerful in the privacy of her own heart."

Miss Blythe listened to her broodingly. "My dear Priscilla," she said, "you could be describing yourself."

"Oh, no." Priscilla laughed and set down her empty cup and saucer beside her. "I am contented with my life, Miss Blythe. There are many thousands in worse state than I. It would be wicked of me to complain."

Miss Blythe sighed again. "You have the gift of contentment," she said. "You always did, even as a child, I remember. And it seems here that every casual client soon wishes to become your regular. You must flatter them into feeling that you enjoy giving them service. Men do not like to return to girls who treat them with disdain or indifference even if they have been gifted with voluptuous bodies."

Priscilla looked down at her own slender form. "When I embarked on this profession," she said, "I decided that the only way I would be able to reconcile my conscience to what I was doing would be to do it as well as I am able. Gentlemen come to me for pleasure. I try my very best to give them pleasure."

"Angela will be waiting, dear," Miss Blythe said. "And I am anxious to question her about the swelling around her eye. Send her in, will you?"

Priscilla crossed the room to set her cup and saucer on the tea tray and bent to kiss the offered cheek of her employer.

"I have another of the same author's books that you must read when you have finished this one," Miss Blythe said before the girl left the room.

Priscilla tidied her room, though a maid had been in to clean already, and turned down the bed carefully to be ready for her first client late that afternoon. Then she took her book and her embroidery downstairs to the girls' parlor — the book to read if she could, the embroidery to stitch on if some of the other girls were there and wished to talk.

She would have liked to go out again to stroll in St. James's Park and drink in the sight of all the spring flowers, but it was difficult to find any girl willing to go out walking on a cool day even though the air was invigorating. Sadie accompanied her on an early morning walk most days only because Miss Blythe had told her that she must keep her weight down if she hoped to remain in the house. Poor Sadie had been forbidden any sweets, except a few on Sundays.

She missed the country, Priscilla thought, settling herself in the parlor and taking out her embroidery despite the fact that only Theresa was present. She was sleeping, her head thrown over the chair back, her mouth slightly open. Especially now that spring had come, Priscilla missed the country.

And she missed her father. And Broderick. They had been a very close family after her mother's death when she was ten. So close that she had been in no hurry at all to marry, even though she had had two quite eligible offers. She had had some notion that she would wait until she fell in love, until she met someone who measured up to her father or her brother.

That time had still not come when she was twenty-two the previous autumn and her father had neglected a chill taken during a hunt and died of pneumonia, all within the span of three nightmare weeks. Broderick would provide for her, he had assured her with almost his last breath. It had all been arranged a long time before. Broderick was in Italy at the time.

He had been summoned in haste. But before the message of his father's passing could possibly have reached him, the message of his own death of typhoid had reached Priscilla. And Broderick, only twenty-six years old at the time of his death, had left no will.

Everything had passed to Priscilla's cousin, Mr. Oswald Wentworth. Everything. Even those more valuable personal possessions of Priscilla's own that her father had had in his own safekeeping. And Oswald and his wife had made her life miserable, treating her a little worse than they treated the servants. The servants at least earned their keep, Irene had been fond of saying.

A difficult, near-impossible situation had finally become unbearable when Oswald had begun to treat her indeed like a servant — or as some gentlemen treated their female servants anyway. It had not been safe to be in a room alone with him, she had discovered, or to meet him in a deserted corridor. He had begun to touch her, to kiss her, to whisper lewdness in her ear.

In the end there had seemed to be only one thing to do — leave. She had made hasty plans to join her former governess, with whom she regularly corresponded, in London. Miss Blythe would give her a position as a teacher or assistant in her finishing school for young ladies, she was convinced. Or else Miss Blythe would use her influence to have Priscilla taken on at another school.

If she left, Oswald had made quite clear and Irene had echoed, she must never expect to be welcomed home again. She must expect no further support from him. She had left.

It was only when she had arrived unannounced on Miss Blythe's doorstep and been shown into Miss Blythe's sitting room that she had discovered that the finishing school her former governess's letters had spoken of was in reality a whorehouse.

Theresa snored suddenly and awoke with a start.

"Oh, Prissy," she said, stretching. "Are you busy again? You are always busy."

Priscilla smiled. "It is my way of relaxing," she said. "Are you tired?"

"Of living," Theresa said. "How do you manage always to look so cheerful? Sometimes I think I might as well throw myself in the Thames."

"Don't do that," Priscilla said, leaning forward in her chair and looking at the other girl with some concern. "Count your blessings, Theresa. At least we have a comfortable home and all our needs supplied. And we know that we will not be overworked or abused here. We know that when our working days are over, we will be looked after."

Theresa pulled a face.

"You need some interest," Priscilla said, "something to occupy your hands and your mind so that you will not dwell on unpleasantness. Really, there is a great deal to be thankful for. Why do you not learn to read? I have offered before to teach you. I am still willing."

Theresa grimaced and got to her feet. "I am going to lie down on my bed," she said, "and sleep while I can. I will be busy enough later."

Priscilla remembered the feeling of being trapped, of being almost totally without options. Oh, it had not seemed quite that way at first. It had been more like a gradually tightening noose about her neck.

She would find employment, she had thought at first. She was quite capable of being a teacher or governess or lady's companion — or even a lesser servant. But employment agencies turned her away — she had no references. Miss Blythe was the only person she knew in London. Her father had been of a retiring disposition. They had never ventured out of the country. An advertisement placed in a newspaper had brought no response. Perhaps Miss Blythe's address — the only one Priscilla could give — was known.

There were no other relatives to whom Priscilla could appeal. No one, though she searched her mind desperately. There had been only Oswald beyond her own family circle. And so the day had come when she had been forced to write to Oswald to announce her intention of returning home. Perhaps, she had thought in some panic, she would be able to signal somehow to one of the gentlemen who had offered for her that she would now be willing to accept his hand.

But she had been given no chance even to try. Her letter had been returned and with it a brief note from her cousin's steward to the effect that Mr. Wentworth did not recognize any responsibility toward indigent relatives.

She had had no home. Nowhere to go. No employment with which to sustain herself. That was when she had felt the noose tighten.

It was also when she had made her decision. Miss Blythe had resisted. She had always been fond of her former pupil, and despite the fact that she ran a strict house and was occasionally severe with her girls, she had a warm heart. But Priscilla had known that though she would not be turned away, there would be an awkwardness about her staying indefinitely as a guest. She would earn her keep, then. Where was she to go if she decided to leave? she had asked an unhappy Miss Blythe. Onto the open street?

Miss Blythe had finally given in after two of her girls, speaking on behalf of all of them, had asked for a private interview and had objected to the fact that they worked while Miss Priscilla Wentworth was a mere parasite in the house.

"And they do have a point," Miss Blythe had said when she had summoned Priscilla afterward. "I am afraid that after all you must face a hard choice, dear. You must leave or you must earn your keep here as the other girls do."

"I will earn my keep," Priscilla had said calmly, feeling the noose choke her. Terror and panic had brought her close to fainting, but she had raised her chin, held on to her outer calmness, and even managed a smile.

"I have never admired you more than I do at this moment, dear," Miss Blythe had said, kissing her cheek — and then turning briskly to business.

And so Priscilla had been put through the careful and rigorous training all the girls received when they first came to the house, except the elocution and deportment classes. And as with the other girls, she had begun work gradually, on a trial basis, one client only each day of the first week.

She did not care to remember that first week.

Finally she had made her life bearable by adjusting to it as best she could. She had always been a cheerful and a practical girl. She worked for only three hours a day at the most. She learned to value that fact. For three hours a day she would work, putting all her training into practice and doing a good job of what she did. She took pride in giving the pleasure for which her clients paid handsomely. She took pride in working as hard as any of the other girls, though it was no secret that she was the favorite.

She was well aware of the advantages of being Miss Blythe's favorite. All her clients were personally chosen for her. She knew that. She listened in some distress to some of the other girls' stories, though of course even they did not have to suffer indignities more than once from the same gentleman. Miss Blythe ran a very strict house indeed.

And when she was not working, she tried not to think about her profession or any of the men who came to her regularly for pleasure. She read a great deal and pondered what she read and sometimes sat for hours with Miss Blythe discussing her ideas. She wrote stories and poetry. She embroidered and knitted and netted. And she painted and played the harpsichord that was kept in one corner of the dining room. She walked outdoors as often as she could and enjoyed the beauties of nature that were to be found in London's parks.

For all of twenty-one hours of each day she was free.

She refused to feel sorry for herself. She had spoken the simple truth to Theresa. She did have a great deal to be thankful for.

She thought suddenly and for no particular reason of her new client of the evening before, perhaps her new regular. Certainly he was going to come again in three days' time.

Sir Gerald Stapleton. The only titled gentleman she had ever entertained. He was a baronet. He was also the youngest gentleman she had had and the most personable. He was the only gentleman ever to have demanded that she lie still, that she be utterly passive in the performance of her duties. Pleasing him had been remarkably easy.

She did not often indulge in fantasies during her working hours. It was one thing that had been firmly emphasized during her training. Work was simply work, a mindless demonstration of certain skills. But she had been a little guilty with Sir Gerald Stapleton. She had lain beneath him imagining that he was her husband, that they were lying on their marriage bed in their own home, that he was begetting their children in her.

At least, for a while she had imagined that, until she had realized how disobedient she was being to her training. She had been taught, and she would have known anyway, that self-discipline was essential if she was to continue to find her life bearable. Her work and the rest of her life must be kept strictly separate.

She had lain still while Sir Gerald slept in her arms during what remained of his hour, and had reminded herself very deliberately that he was a stranger. She knew nothing of him whatsoever except perhaps his tastes in sexual activity. He was merely a gentleman who regularly visited a whorehouse for pleasure, and she the whore who had been assigned to provide that pleasure for that particular evening.

Priscilla folded her embroidery. She opened her book and prepared to enter the world of *Pride and Prejudice.* Yes, there were some forms of fantasy that must be avoided in the future. Now that she had discovered that it was possible — and she had been warned that it was — she must guard against its happening again.

On the whole, she hoped that Sir Gerald Stapleton would change his mind within the next few days and return to Sonia after all.

2

Sir Gerald Stapleton thought himself a creature of habit, much as he hated being so. Sometimes he wished he could be quite free, even of his own nature.

"So you are spending a fortune at Kit's, are you?" his friend the new Earl of Severn said with a laugh.

The two of them were sitting in the earl's library at his town house on Grosvenor Square, where his lordship had taken up residence for a week in order to conduct some business related to his new position. He was in deep mourning for the death of his predecessor and unwilling to appear anywhere in public.

Sir Gerald shrugged. "She has the best girls," he said. "Everyone agrees on that."

"But three times a week, Ger?" The earl laughed again. "You did say three?"

Yes, he had indeed said three. It sounded quite excessive when expressed in his friend's voice. It had used to be once. And then a couple of months before it had increased to twice. In the past few weeks it had been three times, and the days between were beginning to pass with interminable slowness.

"Well," he said, frowning and gazing at the inch of brandy left in his glass, "I vowed a long time ago, Miles, that I would never engage a mistress. She would be sure to get too possessive and it would be too deuced embarrassing to put an end to the liaison. It's simpler just to go to Kit's."

"But three times a week." His friend was doing a deal of laughing, Sir Gerald thought with some irritation. "The same girl each time, Ger?"

Sir Gerald was beginning to wish he had said nothing. Perhaps he would not have done so if the earl had not asked him how Kit was doing. They had used to go there together occasionally.

"Prissy," he said. "She suits me. Does as she is told and all that."

"And for how long have you been wearing a path to her bed?" Lord Severn asked. His voice and his face were still damnably amused, his friend noted.

Sir Gerald shrugged again. "I don't know," he said. "Since spring, I suppose. March, I think it was. I remember her talking about spring flowers the first time."

"For two months." The earl got to his feet, took Sir Gerald's empty glass, and crossed to the desk, on which the decanter had been set. "I am going to have to meet this paragon. Pretty is she, Ger? A lively armful? But need I ask that if you are calling on her three times a week?"

Sir Gerald wished more than ever that he had not raised the subject. He was feeling unaccountably annoyed, though he did not know why. "Pretty, yes," he said. "She suits me, Miles."

"Well," the earl said, handing a full glass to his friend again, "all of Kit's girls are carefully trained to suit any man's needs, if I recall correctly. Devil take it, Ger, it's an age since I had a woman. This being an earl and being in mourning are constraining, to say the least. And my mother and the girls are making ominous rumblings about my duty to the human race, most notably to my earldom. I am going to be shopping at the marriage mart as soon as I throw off these blacks, I strongly suspect. I envy you Kit's and your Prissy."

The conversation moved on to other matters.

But he really had been going to the girl

for all of two months, Sir Gerald mused as he walked home later that night, and far more frequently than he had ever visited any other whore. But Prissy suited him so well. There were no damned tricks with Prissy. No sexual tricks, that was. Of course, there was the trick she had of welcoming him each time as if he were the only man in her life and the only person who really mattered to her. There was a glow, a warmth, about Prissy that made one forget that she was merely a whore plying her trade even when one knew very well with one's head that it was nothing else.

Not that he wanted it to be anything else, of course. He wanted no entanglements whatsoever. He went to Prissy so often because she was just plain damned good in bed. That was all. She was the only woman he had possessed who always did exactly as he directed. All her predecessors had not believed, it seemed, that he was quite unadventurous in his sexual tastes.

Prissy knew now how to please him, and she did just that. So well, in fact, that he had started to see far too much of her. He should call on Kit some time and ask for a different girl. Or he should stay away from there entirely for a few weeks, try another house maybe.

Perhaps he should try celibacy for a while. Except that for all his fear of entanglements, the thought of celibacy was quite unappealing. He needed a greater closeness to another human being than his male companionship could bring. And that could only mean casual physical union with a woman, since he had no intention of ever having any *relationship* with a female.

He had an appointment with Prissy the next evening. He would keep it, and then he would decide whether to call on Kit on his way out to make an appointment with someone else or just not make an appointment at all.

Either way, he was going to have to stop seeing Prissy for a while. If he did not, he was going to feel obliged to continue seeing her forever after and she and Kit were going to take for granted that she was his sole reason for going there. He had broken away from Sonia after three months. Now it was time to break away from Prissy after two.

Except, he thought as he approached his lodgings, that she was so damned good. And it was not even midnight. He redirected his steps to White's. He would see who was there. He would never sleep if he went to bed this early.

His loneliness washed over him and was

pushed out of his consciousness as he entered the club and handed his hat and cane to the doorman.

It had happened at last after almost four months. Despite all of Miss Blythe's care, it had happened.

Two of Priscilla's regular clients were out of town, and Miss Blythe had assigned her to an impeccably dressed gentleman of middle years and quiet manner.

Priscilla had taken him to her room and asked him, as she always did with gentlemen she was unfamiliar with, what she might do to please him. When he had replied and she had informed him that the rules of the house did not permit what he asked, he had raised a hand and smacked her hard across the jaw with the back of it.

She had not called out. During her training she had learned that she must never do that unless her very life seemed to depend upon doing so. She would alert the whole house if she called out and give it a bad name.

She had submitted quietly, consoling herself, as she had also learned during her training, with the thought that that particular gentleman would never be allowed inside Miss Blythe's doors again.

She did not go to Miss Blythe immediately after. She would report on the incident the next morning. She spent far longer than the usual half hour cleansing herself with shaking hands and finally vomiting.

She had another client coming within an hour, she thought as she washed her face and rinsed her mouth and wished that her jaw would stop throbbing. She could not for the life of her remember who it was.

And then she did remember. It was Sir Gerald Stapleton. Oh, thank God, she thought, sinking into a chair beside the fireplace and looking about the room to check that she had not forgotten to turn down the bed. Thank God. She could be sure of courtesy and gentleness with him. She could be sure that there would be no heavy demands on her depleted energies. Thank God it was he.

But the thought had no sooner consoled her than she realized that he was the very last client she wanted to have next. She was too agitated. Her jaw was swelling and darkening.

Not him. Not Sir Gerald. She wanted to be at her best for him. He was the only one of her clients whose visits she unashamedly enjoyed. Despite herself, the fantasies had never stopped in two months. It was a long time since she had even tried to banish them from her imagination.

It was a long time since she had fallen guiltily in love with him.

She did not want him to be next. She would go down to Miss Blythe, she thought, getting to her feet. She would have Miss Blythe tell him she was indisposed.

But she stopped when her hand was on the doorknob. Sonia had been indisposed two months ago, and he had come to her instead. He had never gone back to Sonia. Sonia had complained of it, and had borne Priscilla a grudge ever since. Clearly she had liked Sir Gerald, too.

What if he went to someone else tonight? Angela, perhaps? Or Theresa?

Priscilla bit her lip. Her hand dropped from the doorknob.

But before she could return to her chair, there was a tap on her door and a maid informed her that Sir Gerald Stapleton was awaiting her in the blue salon belowstairs.

Priscilla smiled at him as she entered the room a few minutes later, holding out one hand to him instead of the usual two. She held a handkerchief to her face with the other, as if she had just been dabbing at her nose with it.

"Sir Gerald," she said. "How lovely to see

you again."

"Is it, Priss?" he said, taking her hand and raising it to his lips. "You have a cold?"

"No," she said, lowering her hand and turning away from the light. "Will you come upstairs, sir?"

He followed her up, telling her about a great to-do he had just witnessed in the street when two vehicles had collided and ten others had stopped for their passengers to watch the show and offer their opinions on who was to blame.

"I hope no one was hurt," she said.

"I believe a lady had her bonnet massacred," he said. "But there was no injury more serious than that."

Priscilla closed her door and stayed facing away from him. "Will you unbutton me, sir?" she asked.

"I think I may be going away," he said abruptly as his hands worked at her back. "Tomorrow or the next day."

"Into the country?" she said, her voice warm while her heart plummeted painfully. "How lovely for you, sir. May is the loveliest month in the country, I always think."

"Yes," he said, his hands easing her dress off her shoulders. "Into the country. Tomorrow, probably."

She stepped out of her dress without turning around, and crossed to the bed, where she lay watching him undress, her head turned to the side so that half of her face was hidden by the pillow.

For the last time, she thought, smiling at him. Her throat and her chest were aching with a raw pain. So much for fantasies. She had been right when she had told herself that certain fantasies were dangerous and not to be encouraged. Not that she had seemed to have any control over this particular one.

She lay with her eyes closed a few minutes later, keeping herself still and relaxed as he liked her to be, though not as passive as he perhaps thought her. She had never been quite passive. She had always concentrated on being soft and warm and receptive for him. It had not been difficult since she had fallen in love with him.

He moved his head suddenly and she winced away from him.

He lifted himself on his forearms and looked down at her. She smiled up at him, filling her eyes with warmth as she did with all her clients, though with him it had always been as much unconscious as conscious. He stilled in her, his eyes roaming her face.

"I am sorry, sir," she said. "A little toothache. Let me continue to please you."

He lowered his forehead to her shoulder and drew a few deep breaths before removing himself from her body and from her bed. She watched him walk to the empty fireplace and stare down at it for a whole minute, drawing deep breaths before turning to take up his clothes and dress himself.

Priscilla swallowed. She was unaccountably frightened.

He crossed to the bed when he was dressed and stood looking down at her. She had not covered herself. His eyes moved over her, and he touched her thigh with two fingers. She glanced down and saw the bruise that had developed since she had cleaned herself earlier.

"Where is your dressing gown?" he asked, looking about him.

"In the top drawer," she said, indicating the small chest beside her bed.

He opened the drawer and drew the garment out. "Sit up," he said, and when she did so, swinging her legs over the side of the bed, he held it for her to slip her arms inside. She stood and wrapped it about herself and sat down again on the bed.

"Who did this to you?" he asked, touching her jaw with a light knuckle.

She drew back her head. "It was an accident, sir," she said, smiling at him. "An unfortunate collision of heads."

"Who did it?" he asked.

She licked her lips nervously. "I am not allowed to discuss any client with another, sir," she said.

"He struck you?" he said, and waited for her answer though it was a long time coming.

"Yes," she said at last.

"Why?" he asked, raising her chin with one hand and looking more closely at her bruised and swollen jaw.

"I displeased him," she said.

"You, Priss?" he said. "You displeased someone? Impossible. Why did he do it?"

"What he wanted was against the rules," she said. "He hit me when I refused."

"And then?" She watched his jaw tighten as he clamped his teeth together.

"I did what he wanted," she said in a whisper.

He turned and strode from her room, banging the door behind him.

Priscilla lowered her head into her hands and fought the tears that wanted desperately to come.

Tomorrow she would use the power of her mind to bring herself around again. She had been one of Miss Blythe's girls, a whore, for almost four months, and really it had not been a nightmare of a life, if she discounted that very first time and this night, first with Mr. Farrow and then with Sir Gerald.

All the other days and nights had been at least bearable. She had made a workable life for herself. And it would be bearable again in the future. Mr. Farrow would never be allowed near her or any of the other girls again, and she would get used to the idea that she would not see Sir Gerald again. Indeed, it was as well that he had gone. He had gone while it was still possible to pull herself free from a foolish infatuation. In another few weeks or months perhaps it would not have been possible at all.

Except, she thought, giving in to momentary and uncharacteristic depression, that it did not seem at all possible even now.

She got wearily to her feet and removed her dressing gown again. She had the ritual of cleansing to go through even though Sir Gerald had not released his seed in her.

He had been her last client for the day, she thought with weary gratitude. It was tempting to forgo the ritual or to shorten it so that she could climb back into the rumpled bed and lose herself in sleep. But she patiently and methodically washed and douched all traces of Sir Gerald Stapleton from her body.

Sir Gerald tapped on Miss Blythe's sitting room door since there was no servant in sight to do so for him. He entered at her bidding. She was sitting in her usual place, her spectacles perched on the end of her nose as she peered over them at him, a book open on her lap.

"Ah, Sir Gerald," she said. "What a pleasant surprise. Do come in. You have been calling on Prissy?"

"I want to know who was with her last," he said grimly.

Miss Blythe took her spectacles off. "I am afraid that is privileged information, sir," she said.

"Then perhaps you should go upstairs and examine the bruise and swelling on her face," he said, "and the bruise on her thigh."

The book slid to the floor as Miss Blythe got to her feet. "Priscilla has been abused?" she said. "She has not complained to me, sir."

"Probably because she has been too busy with her duties," he said. "I did not even notice at first. I was too concerned with my own pleasure, I suppose. I want your assurance, ma'am, that she will never be touched by that man again."

"You have it, sir," she said. "I do not allow my girls to be abused. You should know that. Least of all Prissy."

Sir Gerald's hands clenched at his sides. "The very thought of his laying a hand on her is enough to make me want to commit murder," he said.

"It will not happen again, Sir Gerald, I do assure you," she said firmly. "The matter will be looked to immediately."

"She does not have anyone else coming tonight, does she?" he asked.

"No," she said.

"I cannot bear the thought of any other man touching her, either," he said.

Miss Blythe stooped to pick up her book and set it on a table with her spectacles.

"Are your girls bound to you by contract?" he asked. "If Prissy wanted to leave, could she? Or is there a price you would accept?"

"My girls are free to leave whenever they wish," Miss Blythe said. "Most of them never do wish to leave because I look after them well, sir. They are infinitely better off here than they would be on the street."

"I know," he said absently. "If I were to offer to take Prissy away and make her my mistress, you would set no obstacle in the way, ma'am?"

"Indeed I might," she said, "though I have

only my influence to use with her. I would wish to know that her interests would be as well protected under your care as I have tried to make them under mine. Won't you take a seat, sir? I believe we have some business to discuss."

Sir Gerald sat.

Priscilla entered the blue salon the following morning with some trepidation. She had just had a lengthy and painful interview with Miss Blythe, who had told her when it was over that Sir Gerald Stapleton was waiting to speak with her.

He had come to say good-bye, she thought. She wished he had not. She had begun to accustom her mind that morning to the knowledge that she would not see him again.

Surely he did not expect her to take him to her room. The rules allowed no clients in the mornings. Miss Blythe had said nothing about a bending of the rules.

She wished that her jaw were not as black and yellow as it was or her eyes so ringed with dark shadows. She had not slept at all during the night, weary though she had been. And she had been unable to stop at least some of the tears from flowing.

"Priss?" he said, turning from the window

he had been staring through and crossing the room to take her outstretched hands. "Ah, your poor face. I wish I could have stopped it happening, you know, and whatever indignity you were subjected to."

She smiled warmly at him. "Sir Gerald," she said. "You have come to take your leave of me, sir? How kind of you. I do hope you enjoy the summer in the country."

"I have come to take you away from here if you will come," he said.

She withdrew her hands from his and stared at him.

"I have leased a house," he said. "I think you will like it. I have hired two servants and plan to hire as many more. And I have arranged for some furniture. Will you let me set you up there, Priss? Will you be my mistress?"

"Your mistress, sir?" she asked. His mistress? Only him? No others? No daily appointments encompassing three hours and involving three gentlemen? Only him? Only Sir Gerald? He was not going away, after all? She was not to be saved from herself after all?

"I don't like sharing you," he said. "It is distasteful to me. I want you for myself. Will you come?"

Would she come? He wanted her for

himself? He did not wish to share her? There would be only him? Only him!

"You have spoken with Miss Blythe about this?" she asked.

His grin made him look almost boyish for a moment. "She has driven a hard bargain on your behalf," he said. "You must discuss it with her, Priss, and make known to her any changes you wish to make to the agreement. She has it all written out this morning for my signature. She will doubtless read it to you. I think you will find that it protects you from all possible disasters. In particular, you will be well provided for when I grow tir—" He ran a hand through his fair curls. "When we finally part, for whatever reason."

When he grew tired of her. How soon would that be? A matter of weeks? But surely he would not go to the trouble of furnishing a house for her and signing an agreement with her for a matter of weeks. Months, then? Surely not years. He must be close to thirty years of age. He would wish to marry soon — if he were not married already. Her stomach jolted. She had not considered that possibility. But it was a possibility nonetheless.

She smiled warmly. "I am sure Miss Blythe would have had my best interests at heart," she said.

"You will come, then?" he asked.

She had no choice, of course. She conceded that point without even stopping to consider further. She knew that she had no choice even though Sir Gerald would not force her to go, and Miss Blythe would certainly not do so. He had asked her to go with him, to be his mistress, and she knew herself quite powerless to resist. There was no point in going through the pretense of thinking wisely.

"I think I would like to accept, Sir Gerald," she said. "Thank you."

"Splendid," he said, smiling at her. "The house will be ready for you in two days' time. Will that suit you, Priss? I have asked Miss Blythe to release you from your other duties in the meanwhile — provided you accepted my proposition, that is."

"Thank you," she said. "May I see the house before it is ready, sir? Perhaps I can help to set it up."

He scratched his chin. "I would like to have it perfect for you," he said. "But it is to be your house, Priss. If you would like to have a hand in arranging things, then I suppose I could take you there."

"Will you?" she asked, her eyes sparkling at him. "Today, sir?"

"Right now, if you wish," he said. "I have

no other engagements until this afternoon, and I have my curricle outside the door."

"I shall fetch my bonnet," she said, turning toward the door. But she turned back before opening it. "Will you mind being seen with me, sir?"

"If you are to be my mistress, Priss," he said, "I daresay we will be seen together from time to time. I am not ashamed of you."

She smiled and let herself out of the room. She drew several great steadying breaths before approaching the stairs. But before she reached the top, she was running up them two at a time.

She was to be Sir Gerald Stapleton's mistress. There was to be no one else, no more clients at Miss Blythe's. Just him.

3

Sir Gerald followed his new mistress from room to room in the house he had leased just that morning and watched her. She walked quickly and lightly, and she looked about her eagerly, seeing everything. Her cheeks were more flushed than usual, her eyes brighter.

"I will need heavy curtains at these windows," she said when they came to the main bedchamber upstairs. "The sun will shine brightly in the mornings. Not that I mind being awoken early, of course, especially on a day when there is sunshine. This is a pleasant street, sir." She stood looking out through the window. "It seems quiet."

"I chose the neighborhood with care," he said.

She turned and smiled warmly at him.

"This is a cozy room," she said several minutes later, standing in the middle of the parlor downstairs and looking about her. "I like square rooms. They are easier to arrange. And I am glad the fireplace is large. The room will be warm in winter."

He strolled into the smaller room adjoining the parlor. "You will be able to use this room as your private sitting room if you wish, Priss," he said.

She came to stand at his shoulder. "Oh, no," she said. "I think I will make this into a bedchamber. It will be more convenient when I am entertaining you, will it not, just to walk through into this room rather than having to go upstairs. The rooms up there can be my private ones."

"As you wish," he said. "It is to be your house, Priss."

She looked rather like a child with a new toy, he thought. Her dark curls were somewhat disheveled from her bonnet. Her face looked sparklingly pretty if one ignored the ugly bruise on her jaw.

"I have put the choosing of the furniture into the hands of one of my own servants," he said. "If you wish to make any special requests, you had better tell me now and I will let him know."

"But I would so love to choose everything myself," she said. "May I, please? It is a man who is to furnish the house? Men invariably have poor taste and never think of coordinating colors and styles." She smiled impishly at him. "Some men, anyway. I do not necessarily include present company."

He ran one hand through his hair. "Is not a bed a bed and a sofa a sofa?" he said.

"You see?" She laughed at him. "I rest my case, sir."

"Priss," he said, "if you are to be my mistress, I think it would be as well to drop the 'sir,' don't you? You had better call me Gerald."

"Gerald," she said, and smiled at him.

Before they left the house to return to Miss Blythe's, he agreed to send her shopping the next day with Mrs. Wilson, the housekeeper he had engaged for her. He had also agreed to allow her to interview and hire the remaining two servants he wished her to have.

"If they do a poor job," she said with a smile, "I will have only myself to blame since I will have hired them myself. Are you sure you are willing for me to have four servants, Gerald? It seems an excessive number."

"You are my mistress, Priss," he said. "I don't want anyone to be able to say that I don't know how to treat you right."

He was glad the house was unfurnished and there was no opportunity to consummate their new relationship. She somehow looked different from the Prissy he had been calling on and bedding for all of two months. She looked prettier and daintier and more childlike.

She looked like more of a person. He had only ever seen her engaged in her profession. He had not expected that she would be interested in the house and its furnishings or in its staffing. He had expected that she would be interested only in the performance of her duties and the earning of her salary.

He knew nothing whatsoever about her, he realized suddenly. Except her body, of course. He knew that quite intimately — and liked what he knew.

He did not want to know her as a person. He would be glad when she was in residence and he could visit her, as he had at Kit's, purely in order to satisfy his appetites. Except that he would no longer have to make an appointment and his visits would no longer be limited to one hour.

She was his. His personal possession. He liked the thought despite all his earlier reluctance to keeping a mistress.

But he was glad he could not make love to her that day. She was out of her milieu and he was a little uncomfortable with her.

Besides, there was that bruise and the reminder it gave him that she had been regularly possessed by many other men apart from himself. It was a knowledge that he had carefully suppressed until the night before when he had seen the physical evidence.

He did not like the thought.

"I do like it, Gerald," she said as she tied the strings of her bonnet in the hall and he picked up his hat and cane. "Thank you and for the offer you made me this morning. I will try my very best to please you for as long as you choose to employ me."

"You always have pleased me, Priss," he said. "You are good."

"Are you not leaving town after all?" she asked.

"Not just yet," he said. "I'll go into the country for the summer. But you will be able to stay here, Priss. I have leased the house for a year."

She smiled at him and preceded him through the door.

The Earl of Severn was laughing — again. He had seemed to do nothing but laugh since his return to town, Sir Gerald thought.

"So you have set her up in a love nest, Ger," the earl said. "She must be something, this Prissy of yours. You must take me to meet her before I return to the country next week. Will you?"

"I suppose I could arrange that," Sir Gerald said. "But I have told her it is her house, Miles. I would have to have her consent first."

"Of course," the earl said. "Your timing was poor, though, Ger. I was going to come to Kit's with you the next time you went. Who is there these days? Is Rosemary still with Kit?"

"She left ages ago," Sir Gerald said.

"Ah," the earl said. "An interesting girl, Rosemary. I suppose I shall remain celibate and do honor to this mourning." He looked down at his black clothes rather ruefully.

"The thing is," Sir Gerald said, running one hand through his hair, "that I intended to put an end to it last night, Miles. I was going to change to a different girl or leave there altogether for a while."

The earl laughed. "After visiting her three times a week for the last two months?" he said. "It sounded to me as if you were pretty keen on her, Ger."

"That's the trouble," Sir Gerald said. "I don't intend to get pretty keen on any female. As soon as they get wind of it, they get their fangs in. And then you are lost forever. I hate women. It's just too bad they are necessary to one's well-being."

"Ger." Lord Severn got up from behind the desk in his library and strolled to the fireplace, where he set one elbow on the mantel. "Females make up at least half of the human race. Is it not a little nonsensical to generalize about them, to believe they are all the same beneath the skin?"

"They are," Sir Gerald said fervently. "They like to own and possess. They like to pretend to tender feelings, but in reality their own comfort is the only thing of any importance to them. They are clever, vicious schemers. Trust a woman and you are lost for life."

The earl clucked his tongue. "Yes, they do like to manage," he said. "Witness my mother and my sisters, for example. But usually it is a benevolent despotism, Ger. They have this enormous compulsion to try to arrange for the happiness of the men in their lives without ever thinking to consult the man's wishes first. But there is no particular malice in most of them."

"I shouldn't have done it, anyway." Sir Gerald got abruptly to his feet and crossed the room to the window. "She has already had me take her to the house and agree to let her choose the furnishings tomorrow.

And she has already decided that our bedchamber will be the room adjoining the parlor instead of the master bedchamber upstairs as it should be. It will be more convenient, she said."

"And it probably will, too," the earl said, laughing again. "Desire can cool quite abominably in the passage from downstairs parlor to upstairs bedchamber, Ger. One must make the choice between a cooled desire or a hard bed on the parlor floor. Your Prissy sounds like a sensible wench. And you did tell her that the house is hers, did you not say?"

Sir Gerald frowned. "I would not have done it if some oaf had not cuffed her and bruised her," he said, "and forced her into some perversion she would not give me the details of. I saw blood, Miles, I swear, and look where it has led me."

"Whores have to take their chances," the earl said. "It comes with the profession. And Kit would have seen to it that it did not happen again. I don't believe you would have reacted the same way with any other girl, Ger. You fancy this girl. You might as well humor yourself and do her a favor. Becoming a mistress is a step up in the world, after all. Enjoy her while you have her."

"But how am I to get rid of her?" Sir Gerald asked.

"Think of that when you finally weary of her," Lord Severn said with a grin. "A good fat settlement and some sparklers for the throat or ears usually do the trick quite nicely, I have always found. It is something of a blow to one's pride, but most girls are quite happy to be handed on to someone else after a while."

"Kit has made me sign an agreement that looks after the settlement," Sir Gerald said.

The earl threw back his head and laughed. "Good old Kit," he said. "She treats her girls rather like daughters, doesn't she? Your Prissy must be a favorite of hers."

"*The* favorite, apparently," Sir Gerald said with some gloom. "I really do feel quite trapped, Miles. It was almost like signing a marriage contract."

"Well," his friend said, "you have to remember, Ger, that in reality it was no such thing. I wish I could go to the races. Would you care for a ride out to Richmond just for the mere sake of a ride?"

"Why not?" Sir Gerald said with a sigh. "I can't go to Priss until she leaves Kit's the day after tomorrow. It would look a trifle impatient, wouldn't it?"

His friend laughed again and clapped him on the shoulder.

"Ger," he said, "I can hardly wait to meet the girl."

Priscilla could not remember a happier day since before the deaths of her father and brother. She had been frantically busy, seeing to the arrival of the furniture and draperies and carpets, directing workmen as to their placement, using her own meager strength to move furniture that after all did not look quite right where it had been first placed, arranging draperies into pleasing folds, interviewing half a dozen girls for the two positions available on her staff.

She had had a bath and washed her hair before dinner and had put on the rose-pink evening gown with the flounced hem that had always been her father's favorite, though it was now woefully old-fashioned. Her bruise, she had been happy to see at an anxious glance into her mirror, had faded to a dull yellow.

She wandered through from the master bedchamber with its simple furnishings to the smaller bedchamber next door, which was furnished only with a chair and table and easel. Her few books were beside her bed in the bedchamber. Her paints and paper and pens and needlework were in the smaller room, which she had named her workroom.

This would be her private world, the world Gerald would not see, the world she would inhabit when not working. She felt thoroughly happy as she looked about her. She had not had a private world at Miss Blythe's even though she had been fortunate enough to have several hours of every day to herself, alone in her room. But the room had been the same one in which she had done business for three hours of each day.

Now her two worlds could be kept separate. She felt almost like a real person again. She felt less dominated by that oppressive label that reduced her to only a body to be used for men's pleasure. She felt less of a whore.

She looked about her one more time with pleased satisfaction and turned to the stairs. Gerald had left a message that he would call on her during the evening. She did not know the exact time, as she had always done at Miss Blythe's. But it did not matter. She loved the downstairs, too, and had spent more time and money on its furnishings. She had wanted her work environment to be a pleasant one.

She had wanted it to please him.

She stood up when she heard the knock on the outside door and waited for her manservant to answer it and to announce her visitor. She held out her hands to him.

"Gerald," she said. "How lovely to see you."

"Hello, Priss," he said, taking her hands and squeezing them. "You have settled in, then?"

"As you see," she said. She twirled about, her arms extended. "What do you think?"

She had not been extravagant. Everything had been chosen very carefully with an eye to comfort and color and economy. He had given her carte blanche when she went shopping, but she had not wanted to waste his money. She did not know how wealthy he was. Besides, money was never to be wasted.

"Very pretty," he said. "I see what you mean about color, Priss. The greens all blend together, don't they?"

She smiled at him. "Like a spring garden," she said. "Is it not cozy? Will you come through to the bedchamber?"

It was decorated in blues, as her room at Miss Blythe's had been and her room at home. But this was her favorite room of the three because she had chosen everything herself. It was simply decorated but cozy, she thought. Even the coverlet on the bed was a delicate blue. She had turned it down.

"I like it," he said. "You have done well, Priss. And it is convenient, as you said."

"May I offer you refreshments?" she asked.

"No," he said, turning to her. "I just came from dinner at White's."

She felt a little awkward with him. It was different somehow. She smiled, deliberately injecting that warmth into her expression that she had practiced so carefully during her training and used throughout her working hours.

"You wish to go to bed?" she asked.

"Yes," he said.

She turned, comfortable again now that their encounter had taken its usual turn. His hands worked at her buttons.

"This is pretty," he said. "Is it new?"

He had given her an allowance for clothes, part of the agreement that Miss Blythe had drawn up.

"No," she said. "I have had it for ye—" She stopped herself. "I bought it when I started to work for Miss Blythe. I am able to wear it now that the weather is warmer."

She slipped out of the dress and turned to him. As usual during her working hours, she wore nothing beneath. She smiled at him again, without conscious effort this time. And she was struck by the thought that for tonight and for as long as he chose to employ her he would be her only client. And she had always found it easy to please him, partly because his demands were so few and partly because in pleasing him she pleased herself.

She lay down on the bed and watched him as he undressed. She liked his body. He was not particularly tall or particularly handsome or particularly muscular. He had none of the attributes of the ideal man of most girls' imaginations. And yet he pleased her. To her he was beautiful. She reached out her arms to him as he approached the bed and prepared to accommodate her body to his.

"Come," she said, as she had not said since their first time together, "let me give you pleasure."

"In the usual way, Priss," he said, and she closed her eyes, set her hands flat against the mattress, and raised her knees as he mounted her.

"Mm," he said almost an hour later, waking and turning his face into her hair. "It's time for me to go, Priss."

"As you wish," she said, her fingers playing with his soft curls. "But your time is no longer limited to one hour."

"So it isn't," he said, rolling off her and

lying beside her on the bed, something he had never done before. He lay there looking at her. "It is a comfortable bed."

"Yes," she said, smiling at him and settling the blankets up over his shoulders again.

"I should go," he said.

She said nothing for a while but just enjoyed the feeling of lightness caused by the removal of his body from hers. She enjoyed seeing him lying there beside her and reveled in the luxury of knowing that she did not have to hasten him on his way in order to prepare herself and the room for another man.

"Gerald," she said, "I have had so much enjoyment in the past two days. You cannot imagine. It was like a dream come true to have a whole house to furnish yesterday." She laughed. "I don't believe Mrs. Wilson enjoyed herself, though. Her tastes are very different from my own. She wanted me to decorate this room in scarlet. She thought it would be what you wished. In scarlet! Can you imagine? You would not have liked it, would you?"

"I like it as it is," he said. "It is more you, Priss."

"I don't believe I would be able to bring myself to entertain you in a scarlet room," she said with a laugh. "I would feel like a wh— Well, I would feel uncomfortable."

"I would not have liked scarlet," he said. "You were quite right, Priss."

"Well, there," she said. "It is as I told Mrs. Wilson. I have known you for two months, I told her. I know how to please you. I had so much fun today, Gerald. I had the workmen put everything where I had imagined it going, and then I could see that almost nothing was right after all. So I moved everything until it was all just so."

"I hope you did not move anything alone," he said.

"Mr. Prendergast helped me with the heavier pieces," she said. "But I had the feeling that he was impatient with me." She laughed. "Not that I allowed that to deter me. I wanted my house to be just perfect. And I wanted it to be perfect for you so that you will be happy here."

He reached out a hand to cup one of her breasts and stroke its peak with his thumb. He had never touched her there before.

"You have done well, Priss," he said. "You are a good girl."

She smiled and swallowed against the ache his hand was sending up into her throat.

"May I bring a visitor one afternoon?" he

asked. "I have a friend who wishes to meet you."

Her stomach performed a somersault. A friend? Wanted to visit her? She searched his face for a clue to his meaning. But he had said that he did not wish to share her any longer.

"The Earl of Severn," he said. "He wants to meet my new mistress, Priss. He is in town for only a couple of weeks. He is in mourning for the old earl and will be back in the country soon. We have been friends since university days. May I bring him? I told him the decision would be yours, since this is your house."

She still was not quite sure of what he meant by a visit, but she could hardly ask him.

"Yes," she said. "Tomorrow, Gerald? Is he like you?"

"Alas," he said, smiling ruefully, "he is probably the most handsome man in all England. Not like me at all, Priss."

It had been a foolish question. No one was ever like anyone else. And no one could be quite like Gerald. He was one of a kind. She cared not at all for the most handsome man in England.

"Will I be expected to swoon at his feet, then?" she asked, laughing at him.

He grinned back. “Only if you really wish to impress him,” he said. “Otherwise a simple ‘how d’ye do’ will suffice.”

His hand had moved to her shoulder and was rubbing warmly down onto her arm. And then it was at her waist, turning her onto her back again, and he was moving over her and pushing her legs wide with his knees once more.

“Just lie still, Priss,” he said. “I really should be leaving.”

She set her hands lightly at his hips, closed her eyes, and concentrated on breathing slowly and evenly. Sometimes the hardest thing in the world was to lie still and relaxed. Her inner muscles wanted to contract, to draw him more firmly into her, to draw pleasure inward. Her legs wanted to lift from the bed to hug him more closely. Her hands wanted to press more firmly, to feel his rhythm and make it her own.

She lay still and relaxed, breathing slowly, ignoring the spirals of desire that curled upward from the area of his activity through her womb and into her breasts and up into her throat and behind her nose.

“Ah,” he said at last, a world of satisfaction in the sound.

She moved her hands upward to rearrange the blankets about his shoulders. She slid her feet down the bed so that her legs lay flat on either side of his. And she turned her face until she could feel his cheek against the top of her head.

She was in the parlor waiting for them, Sir Gerald was told the following afternoon, when he arrived at his mistress's house with the Earl of Severn. He was glad of that. He was glad that she did not have to be summoned from the rooms upstairs. She had not offered the evening before to show him those rooms.

She was looking very pretty, he thought with some pride when they were admitted to the parlor by Prendergast. She was standing in the middle of the room, wearing a light sprigged muslin dress, her dark curls freshly brushed, that natural blush of color high on her cheekbones. She did not, as she usually did, hold out her hands to him. She looked at him rather uncertainly, a smile on her lips.

"Priss," he said, striding toward her, carrying the hand she finally lifted to him to his lips. "How are you?"

Her smile grew in warmth.

"I have brought the Earl of Severn to meet you," he said. "This is Prissy, Miles."

She curtsied to his friend and blushed. All

women blushed when they laid eyes on Miles. It was his height that did it, damn him, and the breadth of his shoulders, and his blue, blue eyes and thick dark hair.

"Prissy," the earl said, crossing the room toward her, his hand outstretched for hers. "I have heard such glowing reports of you from Gerald that I had to meet you for myself."

His blue eyes were twinkling at her, Sir Gerald saw with an annoyed glance. The earl bowed over her hand and kissed it.

"Thank you for receiving me," he said. "I gather that you gave your consent to Gerald last night."

"Won't you take a seat, my lord?" she said. "I shall ring for tea. Gerald, please sit down."

Tea and cakes were brought in, and she proceeded to entertain them both for the next half hour, doing very little talking herself, but asking skilled questions that kept them — particularly Lord Severn — talking.

Both men found themselves remembering stories from university days and laughing over them. His mistress's eyes were dancing, Sir Gerald saw. He glanced at his friend. She was looking altogether too pretty.

He had never held a conversation with her or in her presence. He would have thought her incapable of sustaining one. A man expected his mistress to have only one set of skills and one body of knowledge.

His Priss had obviously been very well trained indeed by Kit. Her accent and her manners did not slip even once.

He raised her hand to his lips again when he and his friend rose to take their leave. "Thank you, Priss," he said. "I shall see you tomorrow evening?"

She smiled at him.

The earl cleared his throat. "I can see myself on my way, Ger," he said. "I don't expect you to leave with me." He bowed. "Thank you for entertaining me, ma'am. This has been a pleasant half hour, and I believe I can see why Gerald is so taken with you." He grinned and winked at her.

"Devil take it, Miles," Sir Gerald said when they were outside the house and on their way to Grosvenor Square, "can't you allow a man to decide for himself when he wants to mount his mistress? I was with her all last night."

And had her three separate times before finally setting his feet in the direction of home at some time after dawn, he thought.

"She is remarkably pretty and amiable,"

the earl said. "I don't wonder that she was Kit's favorite, Ger. Who is she? No common milkmaid or street urchin, at a guess. A gentlewoman down on her luck?"

"How the devil should I know who she is?" Sir Gerald said. "It's nothing to me, Miles. She is my mistress. She has one function in my life. I have no intention of complicating matters by trying to find out who she is — or was."

"And yet," the earl said, "I would guess that she would be well worth getting to know, Ger."

Sir Gerald stopped walking abruptly. "If you are planning to get any ideas, Miles," he said, "you had better tell me right now and I'll take a jab at your nose before I can remember that you could probably grind me to powder without even exerting yourself. You will keep your mind and your hands off Prissy if you know what is good for you."

The earl chuckled. "Relax, Ger," he said. "I would not dream of poaching on your territory, my friend. Besides, your Prissy is far too sweet and wholesome for my tastes. My tastes run to far more voluptuous wenches. I regret Rosemary more than I can say. She doubtless got herself thrown out of Kit's for refusing to work within the rules.

Kit and her rules!"

"I am very thankful for Prissy's sake that she has them," Sir Gerald said fervently while his friend turned his head and laughed at him again.

4

Priscilla had a delightful feeling of freedom and well-being. She was strolling in Hyde Park at sometime earlier than the fashionable hour, breathing in the warmth and the smells of early summer, gazing about her at the smooth green lawns and up at leaf-laden trees.

She had been to the library and taken out a subscription. And no one had pointed a finger at her and told her she had no business in such a respectable establishment. The librarian had been courteous and friendly. She had a book by Daniel Defoe tucked under one arm. She was swinging her reticule with her free arm.

The walk through the park was an extra treat she had granted herself in honor of the beautiful weather. She thought with some nostalgia of the roses at home. But Hyde Park was quite lovely, too.

She walked a little to the side of the path

as even at that hour there were carriages out and horses. It seemed that the summer weather was drawing people outdoors even before the hour for the usual daily promenade.

She thought guiltily of how Miss Blythe would scold her for being out alone. But those days of having to live by rules, just like a schoolgirl, were over. She was free again and enjoying her freedom.

She had Gerald's visit to look forward to that evening, the first in almost a week. He had not called on her at all during her monthly period, but he would be there that evening. She had missed him.

She had lived upstairs for the whole week, painting remembered scenes of home, singing to herself the remembered songs, which her father had so enjoyed hearing, working at her embroidery, writing poems — love poems, the first she had ever tried — and reading the last of the books Miss Blythe had loaned her.

It had been a happy week even though she had missed Gerald. The week before that, her first in her new house, he had visited her three times apart from the call with the Earl of Severn and stayed for several hours each time, all night the first time. She had liked the arrangement. It was more like having a lover and less like having an employer.

She liked to think of him as her lover. She still had fantasies of him as her husband, of course, but those thoughts were just that — silly fantasy, delightful during the times when he was with her, perhaps, but not to be dwelled upon.

The idea that he was her lover was fantasy, too, of course, but less unrealistic than the other.

Two riders were slowing their horses on the path as she approached. A barouche was coming from a distance away and a curricle coming up behind her.

"Well, good day to you, darling," a gentleman said from his horse's back, raising his hat to her.

Priscilla looked up, startled.

"Are you going my way, sweet?" he asked while his companion chuckled. "My horse's back is broad enough for two."

"No, thank you," she said, continuing on her way, scorning to hurry.

"She is one of Kit's girls," the other gentleman said. "Prissy, isn't it?"

"What?" the first gentleman said. "And escaped from Kit without a leash? You will be in for a spanking when you return, darling."

Priscilla glanced up again and saw that

the second gentleman was a one-time client of hers. He winked at her.

She walked on. The curricle came up behind her and passed. A gentleman was at the ribbons, a young boy in the high seat beside him.

"I don't think she wants a ride, Clem," the second gentleman said. "A shame, ain't it? She might as well enjoy herself, one would think, if she is in for a spanking anyway. I have heard that Kit has a very heavy hand."

"Shall I come home with you, darling, and speak up for you?" the first gentleman asked.

But they were merely two gentlemen having their fun. They turned their horses with a laugh when they saw that she was not going to play along with them and proceeded on their way as the barouche came up to them. Priscilla glanced up as she walked on.

She did not catch the eye of Sir Gerald Stapleton only because he was looking straight ahead. There was a young lady seated beside him, holding to his arm. A young lady who looked at Priscilla in some disdain and said something to her companion.

They were past her and on their way so quickly that she was left wondering if it had all been a dream. But it really had happened and totally ruined her mood.

Who was the young lady? she wondered, alarmed at the stab of intense jealousy she felt. She really knew nothing at all about Gerald's life. She still did not know for sure if he was married or not, though she guessed not if he had so much time to spend with her, unless his wife lived out of town.

Was the young lady his wife? His betrothed? The lady he was courting? She supposed that he might be thinking of taking a wife even if he was not married. He must be close to thirty years of age.

She wished she had not seen them together. She wished she had not walked in the park.

He was not ashamed of her, he had said. But of course she was not to be acknowledged in any way when he was with a respectable young lady — a lady who had never been forced to sell herself in order to live.

Priscilla did not pursue the thought. It was against her nature to give in to self-pity. She had survived, and really she had done quite well for herself. She had no great cause to complain.

But a little of the sunshine had gone out of the day.

■ ■ ■ ■

Sir Gerald was still in a fury when evening came. The week had seemed interminable. He had awoken that morning with a sinking feeling about the planned events of the day but with a lifting of the spirits when he had remembered that he would be able to call on Priss again that evening and every evening if he wished for another month without interruption.

He had paused in the act of shaving, wondering how girls like Priss kept themselves from becoming pregnant. He had not given the matter a great deal of thought before. But somehow they did it. Doubtless they knew tricks that he was unaware of.

He had not been looking forward to the day. He had attended a ball the evening before — one of the infernal events of the Season that he had felt obliged to show his face at. Before he had been able to escape to the card room and a relatively pleasant evening, he had met an old acquaintance of his father's and the man's hopeful daughter hanging on his arm.

He had danced with the daughter and had found himself somehow being drawn into inviting the girl to go driving with him the following afternoon. That was the trouble with females, he had always found. They could trap one into doing things one had had no intention of doing and could leave one wondering how it had all happened.

He did not enjoy driving out with young ladies. There was too much danger that their wiles would trap him into some other commitment.

Miss Majors had been clinging to his arm, confiding all sorts of secrets about bonnets and feathers and fans in her breathless voice. He had been aware that he had brought her out too early and had been sorry for the fact. If he had chosen the more fashionable hour, there would have been a press of other carriages to stop for and a whole arsenal of other people to converse with.

He had been concentrating on the conversation, not allowing his thoughts to move ahead to the evening. He had not wanted to be trapped into saying something impulsive. The girl had been dropping hints about her eagerness to visit Vauxhall Gardens one evening. He had carefully avoided taking the bait.

And then, glancing ahead to the trollop who was flirting with the two dandies on horseback, and annoyed that he was escorting a young lady who ought not to be exposed to such sights, he had become suddenly aware that the girl was Priss and that having spotted him she was walking on, trying to look as demure as a maid.

He had been white with fury.

"I don't think that lady should be out alone, do you?" Miss Majors had whispered to him, drawing her head closer to his. "Papa would not allow me out alone. But then, perhaps she is not a lady. Do you think perhaps she is not, Sir Gerald? How shocking that would be."

He had murmured something soothing and raged inwardly.

He was still in a fury when the evening came. He sat alone at home instead of going to White's to eat, as he had planned. And he ended up eating far too little and drinking far too much. He was late setting out for his mistress's house.

"Gerald," she said, when he stalked into the parlor unannounced. She got to her feet and stretched out her hands to him. "How lovely it is to see you again."

"Lovely indeed," he said. "How long has it been now? Let's see." He set one finger to his chin and raised his eyes to the ceiling. "All of six hours, has it been?"

"Oh, that." She flushed. "They were just

being foolish, Gerald. They were not really harassing me." She lowered her hands when it became obvious that he was not going to take them.

"I'm sorry I came along when I did," he said. "I spoiled your fun, Priss."

"Spoiled my . . . ?" She clasped her hands in front of her. "I was not encouraging them."

"Were you not?" he said. "When you were wearing such a deuced pretty dress and fetching bonnet and were walking all alone in the park? You might as well have had a placard about your neck, Priss, to announce that you were for hire."

"Must a woman walking alone be assumed to be selling herself?" she said. "It was a lovely day, Gerald, and I wanted to feel the sunshine on my face and to enjoy the beauties of nature. I could not help it that there were gentlemen there who were no gentlemen. They were to blame, not I, though they did move away when they saw that I was not interested in their advances."

"You have a maid, do you not?" he said. "Why did you not take her with you?"

"I am twenty-three years old," she said. "I am able to look after myself. If I had had Miriam with me, I would have felt obliged to make conversation with her. Sometimes I would prefer to be alone with my own thoughts. Sometimes I would prefer to be free. Did I embarrass you?"

"You deuced well did," he said. "What would I have done if they had been harassing you, Priss? Jumped down from the barouche and got in there with my fists flying?"

The usual color had deserted her face, he saw when he glared at her. Her jaw was tight.

"I would not have expected any help," she said. "I could have looked after myself."

"I suppose one more tumbling would have been neither here nor there with you," he said.

He was immediately sorry. He was furiously angry with her, and with good reason, he believed, but he prided himself on being a gentleman. He thought she was going to slap him and made no move to defend himself. Instead she turned sharply away and hurried from the room — not into their bedchamber.

He sat down on one of the chairs and lowered his head into his hands. Devil take it, but he had never been so angry in his life. And all the forces of right were on his side. But it was just like a woman to turn the tables on him and make him seem the guilty party.

Seem! What he had said to her was vulgar, to say the least. It had also been hurtful. He had meant to hurt her.

He clenched his fist and banged it on the arm of the chair as he got to his feet. The devil! He had known from the start that he was doing the wrong thing. He should never have set her — or anyone else — up as his mistress. He might have known that his life would become hopelessly tangled as soon as he took on responsibility for a female. He should have left her where she was and let Kit worry about her. Kit would not stand for her girls roaming out at will, he had heard.

He had one foot on the lowest stair before stopping to think. He had told her that the house was hers. She had never invited him upstairs.

Devil take it. Hell and damnation!

"Prendergast!" he roared.

The manservant appeared from the nether regions of the house.

"Go upstairs," Sir Gerald said, "or send one of the maids upstairs to ask Prissy to wait on me in the parlor at her convenience."

"Yes, sir," the manservant said, turning back to the servants' room. "I'll send Miriam, sir."

Miriam was the personal maid Priss had hired herself.

He stalked back and forth in the parlor for longer than half an hour before his request was honored. She stepped inside the door and stood quietly there, looking steadily at him. He stopped his pacing.

"Devil take it, Priss," he said, "stop looking at me like that. What was I supposed to do? Ask you if you had enjoyed your walk in the park?"

"Perhaps," she said.

"I'm sorry," he said. "Is that what you are waiting to hear? I'm sorry. I mean it, too. But I'm not sorry I ripped up at you, and I'll do it again, too, if I ever see you with so much as one toe outside the door again and no chaperone in sight. Understood?"

There was a quirk of a smile at the corners of her mouth.

"Gerald," she said, "I am your mistress. I worked at Miss Blythe's for four months. I am no tender bloom to be protected from the evils of the world."

"You are my mistress," he said. "With the emphasis on the *my,* Priss. And I will not have my mistress wandering about in the park or anywhere else alone, looking and behaving like a tart."

"A tart," she said, raising her eyebrows. "Perhaps that is just what I am, Gerald."

"I employ you for my pleasure," he said. "You are mine, Priss. I told you I did not wish to share you. And that includes having you ogled by the likes of those dandies in the park. You want to walk in the park? I'll take you there. But I'll not allow you to go there alone. And I'll have your promise on that, if you please."

She half smiled.

"Now!" he said. "And you will look me in the eye when you give it, too. And there will be dire consequences if I catch you at it again."

"What?" she asked, still with that half smile.

"I don't know," he said. "If you ever get me that angry again, Priss, I wouldn't be surprised, if I were you, to find yourself bent over my knee being thoroughly walloped."

"I promise," she said quietly.

"How do I know I can trust you?" he asked, frowning.

She flushed. "You don't, Gerald," she said. "But I have always done what will please you, have I not? I will do this, too. I promise."

"I could have wrung your neck," he said. "And if I had not had that chit with me, I probably would have done it, too."

"Then I must be thankful that you had her with you," she said.

He was still frowning at her. "It has been a long week," he said.

"Yes."

His eyes roamed over her. "You are wearing that pink gown," he said. "Because I said I liked it?"

"Yes," she said.

"You thought to distract me from giving you a blistering scold?" he said.

She smiled. "I did not know that you would be angry with me," she said.

"Devil take it, Priss," he said, "how did you think I would feel?"

"Don't get angry again," she said.

He ran one hand through his hair and looked at her in exasperation.

"Let me give you pleasure," she said, taking a few steps toward him.

That smile. That sweet voice. He felt instant desire. The witch!

"I can't stay for long," he said, setting one hand at the small of her back and guiding her toward the bedchamber. "I promised a few fellows I would look in at White's and make up a table of cards."

"It will be as you wish," she said, closing the bedchamber door behind them. "I am here for your pleasure, Gerald."

She turned her back on him and he raised his hands to tackle the buttons at the back of her gown.

God, but he had missed her. He wanted her. He slipped his hands through the gaping opening at her back and slid them around her sides and forward to cup her naked breasts before stepping back in order to dispense with his own clothing.

He would stay for an hour, he decided.

It was a lovely day again, and Priscilla had looked several times from the window and sighed. She had taken Miriam with her that morning for a short walk, but the girl had complained almost every step of the way about her bunions. Priscilla had not thought to ask when she interviewed her new maid whether or not she had bunions.

But there was no point in fretting. Her promise had been given the evening before, and she knew she must not set even one toe outside the door. She smiled to herself.

It had not been funny at the time, of course, particularly when Gerald had made that nasty remark about her being tumbled one more time. She was not normally of a volatile temper, but she had wanted for one horrified moment to smack his head right off his shoulders.

Their evening together had never quite resumed its normal course. When they had retired to bed, he had taken her far more quickly and fiercely than usual and had not fallen immediately asleep, but had rolled to her side and lain staring up at the canopy above their heads.

Only one thing had been as usual. He had spoken of leaving, of his obligation to join friends at White's. And yet he had stayed to make love to her in a far more characteristic manner and to sleep until there was a suggestion of dawn in the sky.

Priscilla returned her attention to *Robinson Crusoe* when she found herself wondering yet again about the young lady who had been in the barouche with him the afternoon before. He had referred to her as a chit. Would he have called a fiancée or someone of whom he was fond a chit? She shook her head and began reading.

But no sooner had she become absorbed in the story than there was a knock on the door of her workroom and Miriam was informing her that Sir Gerald Stapleton was awaiting her in the parlor downstairs.

Priscilla jumped to her feet, closed her book, and hurried to the mirror in her bedchamber. She was not expecting him. He had not said that he would come. She was not dressed for him. She hurried downstairs, anyway.

"Gerald," she said, moving quickly into the parlor when Mr. Prendergast had opened the door for her, "I am so sorry I was not here to receive you. What a pleasant surprise."

He took her outstretched hands and squeezed them. "I came to see if there were any toes peeping over the doorstep," he said.

She laughed. "Were you really checking up on me?" she asked. "You do not trust me to keep to my word, Gerald?"

"I told you that if you wanted to walk in the park I would take you," he said. "It is a lovely day again. I have come to take you to Kew."

"To Kew Gardens?" she said, her eyes widening. "You are going to take me there, Gerald?"

"That is the general idea," he said. "You had better run and fetch your bonnet. The straw one you were wearing yesterday, if you will."

She smiled before turning away in order to run up the stairs two at a time while Mr. Prendergast in the hallway below looked disapprovingly after her. Her father had always called her as pretty as a picture in that bonnet.

She was going to Kew. He was taking her to Kew, she told her smiling reflection in the mirror as she tied the strings of her bonnet at a jaunty angle to one side of her chin.

"To the botanical gardens?" she asked him when they were bowling along in his curricle.

"You said you like to see nature," he said. "I am going to show you nature, Priss."

"I have never been," she said. "In fact, I have not been to many places in London at all. I went straight to Miss Blythe's when I came here."

He looked at her sidelong and said nothing. And she felt herself flush. She had never told him or any other man in London anything at all about herself. She did not want to do so. She was content to be Prissy to those men, even to Gerald. If she said nothing to anyone, she could more carefully guard Priscilla Wentworth in the privacy of her own heart. She could the more surely preserve her identity.

"There is a pagoda there?" she said. "And temples?"

"Anything you care to see," he said. "It is a veritable pleasure gardens, Priss."

"But the botanical gardens," she said, "are what I wish to see the most."

It was a magical afternoon. He took her on his arm and they strolled for what seemed to be hours, seeing all that was to be seen. She was enchanted, though she did criticize the buildings.

"The pagoda looks so out of place in an English landscape," she said. "Don't you think so, Gerald? I suppose that in a Chinese setting it would look quite splendid. But such things cannot be easily transplanted."

"I don't know," he said. "I always thought it rather pretty."

"Yes, it is," she said, flashing him a smile. "It is pretty, Gerald. But a little out of place, nevertheless. And the temples are perhaps a little pretentious." She looked at him, amused. "But very picturesque, I must admit."

"Yes," he said. "I have always thought so."

Sir Gerald Stapleton, Priscilla thought in some amusement, was not a man of discriminating taste. But it did not matter. She loved him anyway. Oh, she loved him very dearly.

There was only one brief incident to spoil the magic for a moment. Another group of strollers hailed Gerald and he walked over to speak with them after hesitating for a moment, leaving her to stand on the lawn they had been crossing. He rejoined her after no longer than a minute, and Priscilla looked away from the curious glances of the two ladies and the amused one of one of the gentlemen.

It was a reminder to her that indulging in her fantasy was not at all appropriate to the occasion. She was not visiting Kew Gardens with her husband. She was his mistress and therefore to be kept quite apart from his more respectable acquaintances.

It was not something to become upset over. She was not upset. She would not allow the incident to spoil her afternoon. She had long before reconciled her mind to what she had been forced to become.

"They wanted to confirm that I would be at Lord Hervey's for dinner and with his theater party tonight," he said. "I had almost forgotten about it. I had better get you home, Priss. Have you seen enough?"

"Yes, I have," she said, though in reality she could have walked for hours more, her hand on his arm. "It was very kind of you to bring me, Gerald. I am grateful."

"You need not be," he said. "You are my mistress, Priss. It is only right that I take you about when I am able."

"Thank you," she said.

She was able to return to her book that evening and concentrate on the story. It had been a lovely afternoon. He had returned her to the house and kissed her hand on the doorstep before vaulting back into the seat of his curricle and driving off while she raised a hand in farewell and Mr. Prendergast stood behind her, holding the door open as if determined to prevent her escape.

"I shan't see you for a few days, Priss," Gerald had said before leaving her. "I have got my name included in a deuced house party Majors has organized out in the country for his daughter's birthday. Friday to Monday. One of these long weekend affairs. I'll see you when I get back."

"Have a lovely time, Gerald," she had said, giving him her warm smile. "I am sure you will enjoy yourself."

He had pulled a face.

She was glad he had not wanted to go. A long weekend. Friday to Monday, and this was Thursday. That meant that she could not expect him before Tuesday. Almost a week — again.

But it would not matter, she thought. She could live upstairs for almost a week. She could be Priscilla Wentworth for almost a week.

How she would love to go to the theater, she thought with a sigh as she opened her book. Just once. She would not be greedy about it. Just once when a Shakespeare play was being performed. *As You Like It,* perhaps, or *The Merchant of Venice.*

Just once. With Gerald.

She immersed herself in the adventures of Robinson Crusoe.

5

Sir Gerald arrived back in London rather late on the Monday evening. He was in a thoroughly bad mood. He made his way immediately to White's, where he proceeded very deliberately to get drunk.

For some reason that he could in no way fathom, Majors had conceived the notion that his daughter would do very well as the future Lady Stapleton. And the daughter appeared to have fallen in quite eagerly with the plan.

Sir Gerald had spent the whole of the long weekend determinedly following about and conversing with Miss Majors's aunt and even flirting with her a little. The woman was sixty if she was a day, so a little flirtation seemed harmless. Instead of being deterred, the brother and niece seemed to have decided that Sir Gerald was already making himself one of the family.

He had been invited to accompany them

all to Vauxhall and the opera within the following two weeks. And what could he have done when the invitations were made face-to-face and so unexpectedly that he had not been given even a moment of time in which to think up suitable excuses? He had accepted the opera invitation. The best he had been able to do with the Vauxhall one was to frown, stare off into space, and declare that he was not at all sure that he was not committed to some other entertainment on that particular evening, though he could not for the life of him remember what.

The opera! Devil take it, he hated the stuff. He did not mind music. Indeed, he played the pianoforte for his own amusement when in the country and had once been told to his infinite discomfort that he had some talent at the instrument. But he hated opera. It was nothing but screeching sopranos and tragic heroes and heroines dying with great dramatics all over the stage.

And Vauxhall. The chit would have him up one of the darker, lonelier alleys before he knew it if he did not pay attention every moment of the evening. And the father would be greeting him with an expectant smile at the other end of the alley.

But he would be damned before he would let that happen. He was not going to be trapped into any leg-shackle this side of the grave. He would definitely discover that he had another engagement for that evening.

"Getting a trifle foxed, ain't you, Stapleton?" Lord Barclay commented cheerfully a little after midnight.

"I must be a slowtop, then," Sir Gerald said gloomily. "I expected to be more than a trifle foxed by this time." He raised one hand to summon a waiter.

"Has that new ladybird of yours kicked you out already, Stapleton?" someone else asked.

Sir Gerald examined the liquid in his glass and swirled it about before downing it in one gulp. And that was another thing. Priss. He had scarcely been able to get his mind off her all weekend. He had tossed and turned each night wanting her. He had counted the hours until he could go to her on Monday evening.

He had pictured her standing in the middle of her parlor, small and dainty, her hands reaching out to him in welcome, her face lit up with the pleasure of seeing him. He had pictured the delicate arch of her spine as he unbuttoned her dress, her arms reaching up to him from the bed, the warm and soft welcome of her body beneath his.

Damnation! He should never have done

it. He should have left her where she was. Kit would have dealt with the man who had abused her. Anyway, she was just a whore who must expect occasional abuse. It had not been his concern at all.

Somehow during one of the nights at Majors's, when he had been half asleep, half awake, the pictures of Priss had got all mixed up with pictures of his mother. The warm smile, which extended all the way back into the depths of her eyes; the welcoming arms; the warm, soft body; and the sense of being wanted and welcomed.

His mother had died suddenly when he was eight years old. She had just disappeared. He had not been called to her deathbed or taken to her funeral. It was all of five years later when he had discovered that there had in fact been no deathbed and no funeral. His mother had grown tired of living with his father and had taken herself off to live with her two unmarried sisters.

She had not taken her young son with her or said good-bye to him or written to him or ever sent him any presents or any other token of her love. That meant that she had grown tired of him, too, that she had never loved him, that all her protestations and shows of love had been so much playacting.

There was no real welcome in Priss's face,

either, or in her arms or her body. She was just damned good at her profession — she had been trained by Kit, of course, and Kit was generally recognized as the best. Priss was a woman working for a living and doing a thoroughly good job of what she did.

He must not begin to take the illusion for reality.

He would not go to her, he had decided. He had come to White's instead to get drunk.

"Hey, Stapleton," someone was saying with a laugh, "the brandy is supposed to be poured into the glass, old chap, not on the table."

There was a general roar of mirth as Sir Gerald adjusted his aim.

He would not go to her tomorrow, either, or the next day. She would be expecting him tomorrow. Let her wait. Let her know that she was not an essential, or even an important, part of his life, that he could take her or leave her. Let her know that he led a busy life apart from her, that she had only the one function in his life, and that he did not need that with any great regularity.

Let her know that she was nothing more than his mistress.

Miss Majors, he thought at the same moment as he realized that he had succeeded in getting himself very drunk indeed, brayed when she laughed. He did not like her laugh. And she did it too damned often.

"Hey, Stapleton," someone was saying, "I think you have had enough, old chap. Let me help you home. I'm going your way, anyway."

"No, you ain't," Sir Gerald said, setting his glass very carefully down on the table, which insisted on swaying with a quite irregular motion. "I'm going to P-p . . . , to P-pr . . ."

"To Prissy's," the same voice said. "It is two o'clock, old chap, and you are about as far into your cups as a man can get without drowning in them."

"Prissy's," Sir Gerald said, swaying to his feet. "That's the place. Got to go there. She 'xp . . . She's 'xpecting me."

"Not at two o'clock in the morning," the voice said. It sounded faintly amused. "And she wouldn't enjoy having you vomit all over her, take my word on it."

"Priss won't mind," Sir Gerald said. "She's 'xp . . . She's waiting for me."

And it seemed as if the mere wish had brought it about. He was banging the knocker without stopping at the door of the house he had leased for Priss and wondering vaguely how he had got there and what had happened to the owner of the amused voice. He rather thought that both the owner and the voice had accompanied him onto the street, but he did not know for sure. He did not much care, either, he thought, laying his forehead against the door while continuing to bang the knocker.

"Prender . . . Prendergast," he was saying, "tell Priss to come to me in the parlor, will you? Or is she there? She's 'xpecting me."

"It is half past two, sir," the servant said in a poker voice. "I will inform Miss Prissy, sir."

Sir Gerald rested one arm along the mantel and his forehead on his arm. It would have been rather pleasant to go to sleep, he thought, if the room would just stay still when he closed his eyes instead of floating off into space, taking his stomach with it.

"Gerald?"

His mother's sweet voice. She would put him to bed and tuck him in snugly and smooth away with her hand and her voice all fear of the devils and ghosts that lurked in shadowy corners and in large wardrobes.

"Gerald?" She touched his arm.

"Priss." He turned and caught her up in his arms, arching her slender body to fit against his. Ah, yes. "I didn't have to come, y'know. I could have gone home. But you were 'xpecting me. Didn't want to dishpoint you."

"Gerald," she said, her arms up about his neck. "Did you walk here? All alone? Come and lie down, dear."

"Can't," he said. "The infernal room won't stop spinning, Priss."

"I know," she said. "Come and lie down and I shall fetch you some water and some coffee to drink. Are you thirsty?"

"I'm foxed," he said.

"I know, dear," she said. "I shall take care of you. Come and lie down. I shall loosen your neckcloth and help you off with your clothes."

She took him by the hand and led him into the bedchamber and sat him down on the edge of the bed. And she talked to him in a quiet soothing voice, though he did not listen to the words, and loosened his clothing, and eased him back until his head was lying on a soft pillow. She lifted his legs to the bed. At one point she was telling Prendergast to prepare some coffee and to bring some water in the meanwhile. He was sipping on the water, her arm beneath his neck.

Her fingers felt soothing against his head.

"Deuced room won't stay still," he said.

"It will be better once the coffee has

come," she said.

"I'm going to be sick," he announced suddenly, sitting up sharply.

"I have a bowl here ready for you," she said.

A slim, cool hand stayed firmly against his forehead all the time he was retching up a quantity of liquor.

"Devil take it, Priss," he said perhaps minutes, perhaps hours later. He was lying back against the pillows again, the taste of strong coffee in his mouth. "Why did I come here? This is damned humiliating."

"You are better here with me than at home alone," she said. "Lay your head on my arm, if you wish, Gerald, and try to sleep. In the morning, I will soothe your headache with lavender water and make sure that the house remains quiet."

He turned gingerly onto his side and nestled his head gratefully on her shoulder. He breathed in the warm, clean soap smell of her. He was naked, he realized. She was wearing a silky nightgown.

God, he felt wretched. But she felt so good.

"Priss," he murmured, settling one hand at her small waist, "I missed you."

"And I you," she said.

He felt her lips brush softly against his temple.

He lost consciousness.

She did not see him for five days after the night when he had come to her so drunk that she wondered how he had found the right house.

It was hard. There had been days when she had been working at Miss Blythe's — many of them when she had dreamed of being her own person again, her time her own, her home her own, her body her own. And it was blissful, she told herself often during those days, wandering from room to room upstairs, rearranging her books, restacking her stories and poems, spreading her embroidered cloth over a table to see what it would look like when it was finished, arranging her easel so that the field of daffodils she was painting would catch the light from the window — it was blissful to be able to be Priscilla Wentworth again.

The chambermaid she had hired enjoyed walking, she discovered, and so the two of them sallied forth a few times each day to shop or visit the library or stroll in one of the parks. The only trouble with Maud was that she liked to talk without pause, recounting all the gossip of London belowstairs —

and some from abovestairs, too — in a hurried, confidential manner.

Priscilla decided that since she could not silence the girl or ignore the sound of her voice, she might as well draw amusement from the stories. And so she still enjoyed her walks, though not on the level that she could do so when alone.

She visited Miss Blythe one afternoon and spent four whole hours — neither of them could believe how much time had passed when Priscilla finally got to her feet to leave — talking about books and paintings and poetry and music and a whole host of other topics that had nothing to do with simple gossip.

"Goodness," Miss Blythe said with a smile, "we have not even discussed the weather, Priscilla. Whatever can we have been thinking of to neglect that topic? And such a beautiful summer we are having, too."

"Yes," Priscilla said. "The parks are lovely, Miss Blythe. Have you been out?"

Her old governess looked severely at her. "You are not wandering about alone, are you, Priscilla?" she asked.

Priscilla laughed. "Only once," she said. "Gerald caught me at it and threatened to take me over his knee if he ever caught me again. I believed him. He was furious."

"Good for Sir Gerald," Miss Blythe said. "He is treating you well, Priscilla?"

"Yes." Priscilla smiled. "I have always liked him."

Miss Blythe sighed. "If only circumstances had been different," she said. "But no matter. That girl of yours will be heartily sick of the sight of my kitchen, Priscilla. You had better go and rescue her."

"Your cook will doubtless be the one who needs rescuing," Priscilla said with a laugh. "Maud never stops talking."

It had been a wonderful week, Priscilla told herself. It was almost like old times, except that her father was no longer there. But it had been a hard week, too. Every afternoon and every evening she had expected Gerald but he had not come.

Had he grown tired of her already? Did he regret setting her up as his mistress? Was he embarrassed by the memories of that night, when he had vomited three separate times into the basin beside the bed and talked drunken nonsense for much of what remained of the night? Had he remembered calling her his mother once? Did he find it hard to face her after spending the morning and part of the afternoon on the sofa with his head in her lap while she had bathed his temples with lavender water and smoothed her hand lightly through his hair?

She missed him. It was dreadful. She should rejoice at the week's respite she had had from having to perform the essential function of her profession. But she missed him.

He came back finally quite late on a Sunday evening, when she had already undressed for bed. She heard the knock on the door and stood silently and expectantly in the middle of her bedchamber until Miriam tapped on her door and told her that Sir Gerald Stapleton awaited her downstairs.

She removed her dressing gown and her nightgown with feverish hands and drew on her rose-pink evening gown. She drew a brush through her hair and pinched color into her cheeks. She ran lightly down the stairs.

"Gerald," she said, going to him, her hands outstretched and seeing with some relief that he was not drunk, "how lovely to see you."

"Hello, Priss," he said, squeezing her hands and releasing them. "It must be almost a week, is it? How time flies. I have been busy."

She smiled and a knife she had not known

was lodged in the region of her heart twisted a little.

There was a brief silence.

"Will you come to the bedchamber?" she asked.

"Yes," he said, "that is why I have come. I can't stay long, Priss. I just thought I would look in on you."

"It will be as you wish," she said, closing the door of the bedchamber, beginning the ritual of her occupation.

He said not a word and did not once look into her face until he was leaving. He allowed her to pleasure him in the usual way and took a great deal of time about it, as he liked to do. And he slept on her afterward for almost half an hour, as he had always used to at Miss Blythe's. And then he rose and dressed himself, as he had always done there too, telling her that he had to go.

He looked at her before he left. She was sitting on the side of the bed, wearing a dressing gown, as she had always done at Miss Blythe's. He touched her chin with one knuckle.

"Thank you, Priss," he said. "You are very good."

She smiled warmly at him. "I am here to give you pleasure, Gerald," she said.

He left without another word.

Priscilla sat on the edge of the bed for a long time before rising to begin the cleansing ritual. *You are very good,* he had said. A very good whore. Very good at following directions. Good at opening herself to him and holding herself still for him while he took his pleasure from her body in the way he best liked to do it.

Yes. She had got the message. She was very good at reading messages, too.

There had been two days of rain, but the sun was shining again on Monday. It was a good day for an outing. It was the day he would have been going to Richmond with Miss Majors and a party of her friends if he had not wriggled out of it by pleading a prior engagement, Sir Gerald remembered.

Well, his prior engagement would be with Priss. He would take her to the Tower of London. Doubtless she would be impressed with the Crown Jewels and delighted with the menagerie. Females usually were. And he remembered telling her once that it was his duty to take her about since she was his mistress.

He could permit himself an afternoon out with her, he decided. In the past week he had clearly established to her the real nature of their relationship, if she had ever misunderstood it, though he had to admit that Priss had never ever been demanding, even in the smallest of ways. More important, he had convinced himself in the past week that he could relegate her to the proper place in his life.

There was Lady Leighton's ball to attend that evening and his obligation to dance the opening set with Miss Majors. Yes, he could allow himself an afternoon with Priss.

She was in the hallway tying the ribbons of her bonnet beneath her chin when he arrived.

"On your way out, Priss?" he asked, looking into her startled face. It was the straw bonnet, he saw, the one he liked.

"Oh," she said, "just for a walk, Gerald." She smiled. "With Maud, so you must not frown at me like that. But I will be delighted to entertain you instead." She pulled free the strings of her bonnet.

"I have come to take you to the Tower," he said. "That is a devilish pretty dress, Priss. Is it new?"

"No." She shook her head. "I have had it an age, and it is dreadfully out of fashion, I am afraid."

"I don't know anything about fashion," he said. "Fashion is just to keep the ladies buying, if you were to ask me, and the gentlemen too, if it comes to that. But I do know that it suits you, Priss."

"Thank you," she said. "The Tower, Gerald? Are we going to see the armory and the weapons and the dungeons?"

"Oh, nothing too heavy," he said. "Nothing to addle the female brain. I thought you would enjoy seeing the animals. The elephant is a great favorite, so I have heard."

She was tying the ribbons of her bonnet again. "I would prefer to see the weapons and the armory, if you please," she said.

"Not the animals, Priss?" he said. "There are birds, too, apparently."

"If it is all the same to you, Gerald," she said, "I would rather not. I cannot bear to think of animals being held in captivity. I think they should be free in the wilderness and the birds free in the sky."

"But then no one would ever get to see them close up," he said.

"But in paintings we would," she said, "and in our imaginations. Besides, is it right to deprive another creature of its liberty merely for our pleasure?"

He shrugged. "All the old armor and stuff it will be, then," he said. "I just hope you will not be horribly bored, Priss. How about the Crown Jewels?"

"It would be splendid to see those," she

said, smiling warmly at him. "Are you going to take me there, Gerald? How kind you are."

"Well," he said, "I have to take you about, Priss, don't I? And I was busy all last week." Busy going mad with loneliness and boredom, he thought.

She did not, as he expected her to do, wander quickly through the armory and past all the weapons, picking out only what might be called pretty. She examined everything in minute detail. He would have been mightily bored himself if he had not simply enjoyed watching her absorption and admiring her blue muslin dress, which he could not for the life of him see as being unfashionable. He felt a surging of pride when an elderly gentleman glanced at her once and then returned his eyes for a more appreciative look.

"Oh," she said with a sigh when they were on their way at last to see the Crown Jewels, "so much history, Gerald. We are surrounded by all this richness of our heritage."

"You wouldn't be nearly as fascinated, Priss," he said, drawing her arm through his, "if you had had to read through history books and sit through history lessons as I was forced to do."

She smiled at him. "Perhaps not," she

said. "Sometimes it is an advantage to be a woman of no education, I suppose."

"Believe me," he said, patting her hand, "it is. As soon as we have finished in here, I am going to take you for an ice."

"Are you?" she said. "What a lovely afternoon this is turning out to be, Gerald."

He remembered the night before as he drove her home in his curricle. He had treated her more like the whore she had been at Kit's than as the mistress he had set up in his own establishment. He had been so determined to break from the growing dependency he felt on her during those last weeks when she had been at Kit's and the first little while she had been with him that he had behaved entirely according to a preconceived plan.

But it had not been satisfactory. He had left her house and wandered aimlessly about the streets for hours before returning home to bed and lying awake for another few hours. He might as well have stayed with her as he had wanted to do.

It was late afternoon. He had a ball to get ready for. He should drop Priss off at the door and continue on his way.

"Thank you for a lovely afternoon, Gerald," she said, smiling brightly at him as he lifted her to the ground.

She was such a tiny little thing, he thought. His hands almost met about her waist. And she weighed no more than a feather. The poke of her bonnet did not reach quite to the level of his eyes.

"Will you come in?" she asked him. "I will have tea brought to the parlor."

"It is not tea exactly I have in mind, Priss," he said.

"It will be as you wish," she said, preceding him up the steps as he watched the feminine sway of her hips.

He wondered many minutes later if their beddings brought her any pleasure at all. She always lay so very still and gave no sign or sound at all. He raised himself on his forearms and looked down into her face.

Was there a certain dreaminess in her eyes? he wondered. But if there was, it disappeared immediately to be replaced by the practiced smile, the one whose warmth seemed to proceed from the depths of her soul.

He watched her as he moved in her, pushing himself deep inside her. She held his eyes, the smile fading a little.

"Gerald," she whispered to him, "am I not pleasing you?"

"You are pleasing me very well," he said. "You always do, Priss. You are a good girl."

He continued to watch her after she had closed her eyes. After a while her teeth caught at her lower lip and he knew that his scrutiny made her self-conscious. He lowered his head against her curls and proceeded with his slow lovemaking.

And for the first time he wondered about her, about the life she had lived before becoming a whore, about the forces that had led her willingly or unwillingly to adopt that profession, about her thoughts, her hopes, her dreams.

He should not have come inside the house with her, he thought. The afternoon had been a good one. He should not have brought her to bed when he was feeling pleased with her and even affectionate toward her. He did not want her to be a person to him.

Priss.

Just his mistress, not a person.

He slid his hands beneath her to hold her steady and drove himself to a quick climax.

It was just sex with Priss. Sex for him, business for her.

He felt her twitch at the bedclothes with one foot, as she usually did. The blankets and her arms settled warmly about his shoulders. He turned his face into her soft, sweet-smelling hair and allowed himself to slip into sleep.

6

Life fell into a pattern that Priscilla did not find by any means unpleasant. She had a great deal of time to herself and used every moment of it to be busy. The day never seemed to have enough hours in it. She grew dissatisfied with writing stories and began to write a whole book. And she became absorbed with her characters and caught up in their emotions so that hours could pass that seemed more like minutes.

Gerald came to her frequently, sometimes every day for a week, sometimes with gaps of several days between. She learned to expect him daily but not to live for his coming. She learned to enjoy his company and their physical encounters for what they were worth without giving in too strongly to the illusion that he was her lover, though the illusion was always there in the part of her that she knew to be fantasy.

Usually he stayed for longer than the time

needed for a bedding and the short relaxation afterward — though not always. Sometimes he came in the evening and stayed all night, occasions she came to hope for and cherish without ever expecting.

He never again came to her drunk, though sometimes he arrived after midnight, irritable from some entertainment of the *ton* that he had not wished to attend in the first place. Once he came to her with a red nose and watering eyes and feverish cheeks.

"I can't drive you out to Richmond as I promised, Priss," he said from the doorway of the parlor, waving away her outstretched hands. His voice was nasal and breathless. "I have the devil of a cold. Some other time. I'm going home to bed."

"Gerald," she said, watching him hunch his shoulders and shiver, "there is a bed here. And you have a fever, poor dear. Come and lie down and let me look after you."

"I don't want you to catch it, Priss," he said. "Keep your distance. I'll come back in a few days' time. Maybe tomorrow. I should feel better by tomorrow."

"Did you bring your curricle?" she asked. "I will have Mr. Prendergast see to sending it home for you. Come and lie down, Gerald." She linked her arm through his and led him in the direction of the bedchamber.

He did not resist. "I shall go to the kitchen and fetch a bowl of steaming water for you to set your head over so that you can clear out your nose and breathe again. And while you are doing that I shall mix up a powder for you to drink that will help you sleep. Let me help you off with your boots." She pressed on his shoulders so that he sat down on the edge of the bed.

"I don't want to be a trouble to you, Priss," he said.

She set one of his boots on the floor and tackled the other. She smiled up at him. "You are never a trouble, Gerald," she said. "It will be my pleasure to make you comfortable. I would only worry about you if you were at home alone."

He had never told her that he was not married or that he did not live with relatives. She had drawn her own conclusions from the number of times he had stayed with her overnight without ever seeming to feel uneasy that someone would wonder where he was. He probably lived in bachelor rooms with only a valet for company, she guessed.

He sniffed. "Wretched nose," he said. "I wish I could cut it off."

"You would look funny," she said, cupping his cheek with a light palm as she got to her feet. "I shall be back in just a few minutes, Gerald, and then I shall make you more comfortable. You will be warm and asleep before you know it."

He stayed for two days, two days of bliss for Priscilla. She rarely left the sickroom. He allowed her to fuss over him and hold him and comfort him just as if he were a child.

"You're a good girl, Priss," he said, hugging her briefly when he was finally leaving. "I feel as right as rain again."

"Of course," she said, smiling. "You were the model patient, Gerald."

She caught the cold from him, and the fever. They coincided with the days of her monthly period. She fought them out alone in her bedchamber upstairs so that by the time Gerald came back there was no trace remaining. She did not tell him.

One morning he arrived to take her to a milliner's on Oxford Street to buy her a straw bonnet to replace her old one, which had been ruined when she had been caught out in an unexpected rain shower. And then he took her into a jeweler's to buy her a diamond-and-emerald bracelet.

"But Gerald," she protested, "you don't need to buy me gifts. You provide well for me."

"A gift is just that, Priss," he said. "It is not payment for anything. I want you to have it, that's all. I like to see you with pretty things."

It was a very pretty bracelet. It reminded her of one her father had given her on her eighteenth birthday, one that had been kept for safekeeping with her father's valuables, and one that she had been unable to reclaim after her father's and Broderick's deaths. She had last seen it on the wrist of Cousin Oswald's wife.

"You aren't crying, are you, Priss?" Sir Gerald asked.

The jeweler turned away tactfully and busied himself with putting away the other bracelets they had been viewing.

"Yes, I am," she said with a laugh, brushing a tear firmly from her cheek. "It is lovely, Gerald. Thank you."

"Well," he said, clearly embarrassed, "I think you should possess one valuable thing in your lifetime, Priss." He fumbled in a pocket and handed her his handkerchief.

One evening he took her to Vauxhall Gardens, and she danced beneath the stars and the colored lanterns and ate ham and strawberries and drank wine and watched the fireworks display and strolled along the main promenade, her arm through Gerald's.

It would have been better, she thought, if they had not been members of a party that included three of Gerald's acquaintances and the mistress of one of them. The unattached young gentlemen ogled the ladies around them and openly commented on their physical attributes without regard to the sensibilities of the two women. And the other woman appeared to find everything funny and giggled incessantly.

But she would not allow the company to spoil her evening. Gerald kept her away from them for much of the time. And besides, she reminded herself, she was as much a mistress as the other girl, and she could not expect the other gentlemen to treat her with the same deference they would have accorded a lady.

It was a happy routine that life settled into, though as time went on there was a little desperation involved, too. The Season was drawing to an end and summer was beginning. Gerald always spent his summers in the country, he had told her more than once, at Brookhurst, his home. He was planning to go that year, too.

It was going to be a long, lonely summer. And there was always the very real chance that in the months away from her he would decide that he no longer wanted her. Once he left London, perhaps she would never see him again.

The thought sometimes brought panic, and it always brought a dull ache of anticipated loneliness and pain. But Priscilla had never been one to wallow in self-pity or to allow her spirits to be dragged down with might-have-beens or might-bes.

She counted her blessings. At least she would be able to spend a summer in which she was her own person. If Gerald had not set her up as his mistress, her summer would be the same as the winter and part of the spring had been. She would be at work at Miss Blythe's.

Loneliness was better than that. Her life there, which she had made bearable at the time, now made her shudder in retrospect. It was strange to her that she had ever been able to adjust her mind to a life of such indignity.

The human spirit, she had discovered with some surprise, was capable of carrying one unbroken through even the worst of tribulations. It would carry her through a few months of loneliness and the absence of her lover. And if he no longer wanted her at the end of the summer, well then, she would live for as long as she could on the money she had saved and on the settlement he had agreed to pay her, and then she would do what she had to do to survive until she was thirty years old and able to inherit her mother's fortune.

She would not think of it. The present had troubles — and joys — of its own. The future would be dealt with when it came.

As for the present, he had not left London yet. There was still each visit to be looked forward to and enjoyed. There was still pleasure to give and a little joy to take secretly for herself.

"I have been thinking of getting rid of Lettie," Bertie Ramsay was saying to Sir Gerald. "I want to go to Brighton for a month or so, and m'aunt wants me to trot down to Bath after that — m'uncle's sixtieth birthday or something like that. Sixty-fifth, maybe it is. It seems hardly worth the expense of paying her to wait for me. The girl giggles too much, anyway."

The two of them were viewing the horses at Tattersall's, though neither was buying.

Gerald could sympathize on that last point. He had found Lettie's giggle most irritating at Vauxhall a few evenings before. Priss would never have got out of Kit's or merited a second visit from him there if she had been even half the giggler.

"I know what you mean," he said. "I would probably drop Priss too if I did not have a lease on the house."

"If you ever think seriously of doing it," Mr. Ramsay said, "you had better let me know, Stapleton. I would take her off your hands in a minute. A real lady is Prissy. Good between the sheets, is she? But then I daresay she is. She was one of Kit's girls, wasn't she? Kit always trains 'em well and slings 'em out on their ears if they don't want to learn."

Sir Gerald concentrated on the chestnut mare he happened to be looking at. He did not answer the question. He felt his fingers curling into his palms and flexed them. If Bertie Ramsay imagined that he would ever pass Priss on to the likes of him, he must have feathers for a brain.

"Coming to Brighton, are you?" Mr. Ramsay asked. "Or are you going to Brookhurst?"

"Brookhurst," Sir Gerald said. "I always look forward to getting down there. I don't know why I don't live there all year, in fact."

He did know, he thought almost as soon as he had spoken the words. There were too many ghosts at Brookhurst. Too many damned ghosts.

"Perhaps I'll call on you there," Mr. Ramsay said. "Brighton can get tedious, and who wants to spend longer than he needs to do in Bath with all the octogenarians?" He laughed loudly and merrily at his own joke.

"You would be welcome," Sir Gerald said.

"I think I'll walk over to Lettie's now," Mr. Ramsay said. "There's not much for cattle here today, is there? I have my eye on Spender's grays, but I doubt he will sell them cheap. I think I'll plow Lettie a couple of times and then break off with her. I'll miss that body, I must confess, but it don't hurt to have a change every couple of months or so. How much do you think I should pay her, Stapleton?"

Sir Gerald shrugged. "I suppose that is between you and Lettie, Ramsay," he said. "You would not want to turn her out onto the streets without a decent settlement, though, would you?"

"She don't have to work the streets if she don't want to," Mr. Ramsay said. "She could get some respectable employment instead. There are plenty of jobs for girls in kitchens and such. She does it because she enjoys what she gets from the likes of you and me, Stapleton. All the same they are, the Cyprian breed. Prissy too, if you don't mind my saying so. Quite the lady, she is. Could get a job as some old girl's companion just like that if she chose." He snapped his fingers. "But that would be too dull for her. She would prefer to earn her bread by —" He completed the sentence with an obscenity.

Sir Gerald noticed that his hands were opening and closing at his sides again.

"If you want to go to Lettie, Ramsay," he said, "don't let me keep you. I shall stroll around here awhile longer and see what sells."

"I hate to leave you alone," Mr. Ramsay said, "but I had better get this thing over with Lettie while I have it in my mind. How many handkerchiefs do I have?" He laughed as he patted his pockets. "I am bound to have the waterworks turned on all over me."

Sir Gerald turned away.

Bertie Ramsay was only a chance acquaintance, a friend of Peter West, another acquaintance of Sir Gerald's with whom he had agreed to go to Vauxhall a few evenings before. He had not been looking for any such entertainment, but it was the same evening as he had been asked to go with the Majorses. He had pleaded a prior engagement and had thought that perhaps the opportunity to be seen by them squiring around another young lady was too good a one to be missed. It appeared to have worked like a charm.

When Ramsay had had nothing to do at White's an hour or so earlier and he had had nothing particular to do, either, he had agreed to accompany the man to Tattersall's.

He hoped Ramsay would forget about his plan to call at Brookhurst during the summer.

Sir Gerald left Tattersall's and began to walk aimlessly. He had never thought of his relationship with Priss as anything sordid. Even when he had taken her as his regular whore at Kit's it had not seemed sordid. He was a normal young man with normal appetites, satisfying them in a thoroughly normal way at a whorehouse that had a reputation for cleanliness and skilled girls.

Priss was his mistress, the woman he housed and paid to give him regular and exclusive access to her body and the satisfaction of his needs. There was nothing unusual about such an arrangement. He benefited, Priss benefited, everyone's interests were served, and no one got hurt.

There was nothing sordid about it.

Sir Gerald looked up sharply to find himself the object of a furiously shaking fist and a stream of hair-raisingly colorful language. It seemed that he had crossed a street with his head down and caused a near collision between a gentleman's phaeton and a vegetable cart. It was the carter who was excited. The gentleman was grinning.

"Who is she, Stapleton?" he yelled. "You had better keep yourself alive for her, old chap."

Sir Gerald grinned back at him and raised his hat to the carter.

He could not associate vulgarities like "plowing" and that other one Ramsay had used with Priss and what happened between them in their bed.

Priss was too good to be described in coarse terms. Not good in the way one would expect a whore to be good, perhaps, but good in the way one would expect a wi— . Well, she was good. She satisfied him utterly and always had. Even that very first time she had given him precisely what he had asked for. He could not remember a time when she had failed to please him in bed.

And yet he had told Ramsay in that careless tone men tended to use when talking of women, especially women they used only for sex, that he would have thought of dropping Priss too if he had not leased the house for a year.

Would he? Was he keeping her only because he had paid for the house anyway and might as well get value for his money? Would he drop her if he had to pay out more rather than keep her over the summer so that she would be there for him when he returned to town in the autumn or winter?

Devil take it. He stood still on the pavement and did some mental calculations, frowning down at the ground. It was early July. He would spend the second half of the month at Brookhurst and all of August and September. Often he stayed for October, too, and sometimes for November. Two years before he had stayed until after Christmas.

Probably he would be away from Priss for three months.

He walked on. Three months. Yes, it would be a good thing, too. It would give him time to get his head and his body clear of her. After three months he would be able to see his association with her in better perspective again. And he would keep her over the winter, until the lease ran out the following May. No longer than that. He would begin to feel too tied to her if he kept her longer than a year.

Perhaps he would not keep her so long. Perhaps he would finish with her before Christmas and let her stay out the lease on the house so that she could look about her at greater leisure for a new protector.

Devil take it. He had better look after her, that new protector. He had better not start talking in public about plowing her or anything ugly like that. Not if he knew what was good for him.

Sir Gerald looked up in some surprise at the door of his mistress's house. He had not realized that he was walking in that direction.

"Is Prissy at home?" he asked Prendergast, handing the man his hat and cane when he stepped inside the hallway.

"Upstairs, sir," the manservant said. "I shall send Miriam up to inform her that you are here."

Sir Gerald stepped into the parlor.

"Gerald," she said, coming in no more than two minutes after him. "How lovely."

Priss had the gift or the training always to make him feel that seeing him made her day special. There was always a lightness in her tread, a glow in her face, a warmth in her eyes. He took her hands in his and squeezed them.

"I did not have anything to do," he said, smiling at her ruefully. He had never made that admission to Priss before. Besides, if he thought about them, his words had not been very complimentary. Did he come to her only because there was nothing else to do?

Did he?

"I'm glad," she said. "And so you came to me, Gerald."

"Priss," he said without ever realizing he was going to say what he did, "who taught you to act so much like a lady?"

She smiled. But this time — or was he just fancying things — the smile did not extend all the way back into her eyes. It stopped at a barrier just this side of her soul.

"Miss Blythe, of course," she said. "Have you not heard that she is the best teacher of young women in London, Gerald? I am partial, of course."

"Yes," he said. "You must be her prize pupil of all time, though, Priss. You must be a good learner."

"So she said." She smiled at him again. "And thank you for the compliment, sir."

"I am not surprised that you were her favorite," he said.

"I think all her girls are her favorites," she said. "She cares, you know, Gerald, despite her profession and ours. We are people, you know, we whores."

"Don't call yourself that," he said, frowning. "You aren't a whore, Priss. You are my mistress."

"Yes," she said.

He realized that he still had her hands in his. He released them.

"You came to London from the country?" he said. "From where?"

"From somewhere else." The smile had moved forward in her eyes so that it was quite shallow.

"What did you do there?" he asked. "What did your father do? Your family?"

She shook her head slightly. "I am your mistress, Gerald," she said. "In that capacity I will do all in my power to please you. I have no past and no future. Just this present reality. I am your mistress. Will you come into the bedchamber and let me give you pleasure?"

Her answer gave him a strange feeling of relief. He did not know what he had been about, asking her those questions. If she had answered them, he might have been lost forever. She might have become irrevocably a person to him. Not just Priss, but a person.

Lost forever? He frowned as he followed her through to the bedchamber and shrugged out of his coat. And what the devil did he mean by that?

"I have no buttons today," she said with a smile. "Only pins. I can manage on my own."

She undressed quickly before him as he plucked absently at his neckcloth and the buttons of his shirt.

"You will be pulling your buttons off and incurring the wrath of your valet and your tailor if you tear at them like that," she said, coming toward him when she had stepped out of her own clothes. "You are not usually so careless, Gerald. Let me."

Her smile and her light tone took away any impression of nagging from her scolding. He stood still while she opened his shirt and pulled it from the waistband of his pantaloons. She touched his chest with light fingertips before crossing to the bed and lying on her back in her usual position, waiting for him.

"Priss," he said, "I am going to take you to Brookhurst with me for the summer."

Was he? Was that what he had come here to say?

Her mouth formed an "O."

"There is no point in having a mistress if she is far away from me for three whole months and perhaps even longer, is there?" he said.

He lowered himself on top of her as he usually did, waited for her to adjust her body to his, slid his hands beneath her, and mounted her.

"I don't want to be without this for three months," he said. "It's good with you, Priss."

He heard and felt her swallow.

"Your family?" she said. "Your servants? Your neighbors? Will they not be outraged?"

He had not thought about it. He had never planned to take her with him. He had not given the matter a conscious thought.

"I don't have any family there," he said. "They are all dead. The servants may think what they please. The neighbors can still visit and I can visit them. There are plenty of places for you to go, Priss, where you won't run into them. I'm taking you, anyway. If anyone does not like it, then he can stay away. It won't matter to me. If it comes to a choice between you and the approval of my neighbors, then I'll take you."

He began to move in her and sighed his appreciation against the side of her face. This was exactly where he wanted to be. He wondered he had even thought of Tattersall's or anywhere else when there was Priss to be visited and bedded.

"Gerald," she said, "should I not be consulted?"

He stilled and lifted himself to look into her face. "Why?" he asked. "You don't want to come, Priss?"

"I don't want to be the cause of scandal,"

she said.

He frowned down at her. He did not want to think. His body was aroused for action.

"You will do as you are told," he said. "Should you be consulted? No, you should not. I pay you to be my mistress, Priss, and to do what I tell you to do and go where I tell you to go."

He felt her stiffen.

"I think you sometimes forget that," he said. "Perhaps I give you too much rein."

She stared up at him.

"You will be coming with me," he said, "because I say so. I'll not hear another word from you on the matter."

He looked away from her eyes. He looked at her shoulders, with their creamy skin and delicate bone structure.

"Relax your body for me, Priss," he said.

She obeyed him instantly and he lowered his face into her curls and finished his business with her more quickly than was his habit. He did not enjoy their coupling at all. He was angry. Angry with her for voicing concerns that should have been his own, for pointing out to him all the rashness of his decision. Furious with himself for sounding so much like his father.

For *being* so much like his father. Autocratic. Bad-tempered. Always right. Contemptuous of the women in his life. Treating them as if they were things, not persons.

"Priss," he said, rolling to one side of her almost as soon as he was finished in her, keeping his arms about her and bringing her over onto her side to face him. "Priss?"

She stared blankly across at him.

"I want you there," he said. "I will not be comfortable without you. And I want you in the country for the summer. You will enjoy it, won't you? You come from the country, don't you? I don't see much of my neighbors, you know. Most of the time it will be just you and me. I want you to see it all. I want to show it to you. It's important to me, my home."

She stared at him.

"Will you come?"

"Do I have a choice?" she asked after a pause during which he thought she was going to say nothing.

He swallowed. "No," he said. "But I want you to want to come, Priss."

"Why?" she asked.

He shrugged. "I don't know," he said. "But I want you willing. I don't want you sulking the whole time. I don't want to see you unhappy."

"Gerald," she said. "I try to please you. Not just because you pay me for my favors and not just because you are a man and stronger than I and able to enforce obedience at your will. I try to please you because it is my wish to do so, because I have freely chosen to be your mistress and to satisfy your physical needs. I could have stayed at Miss Blythe's, and I would have done so if I had not wanted to come with you and please you. I don't like it when you speak to me as you spoke a little while ago."

He got up from the bed and began to dress. He turned to her when he had secured his pantaloons at the waist.

"Very well, then, Priss," he said. "The choice will be yours. Come if you will. Stay here if you would prefer. I'll not force you either way. You can have an easy summer if you wish, with no one to please except yourself. You have earned a holiday because you have always pleased me very well indeed and never ever denied me. I shall be leaving in a little over a week's time."

There was a certain impishness in her smile. "I shall be ready," she said.

"To go with me?" He frowned.

"To go with you."

He buttoned his shirt and knotted his neckcloth with careless fingers. "Women!" he said. "I'll go to my grave not understanding them any better than I did the day I was born."

"Gerald," she said, "you cannot go out onto the street looking like that. You would turn every head. Let me tie it for you." She got up from the bed, and his eyes moved over her appreciatively. She did not, as she usually did after their couplings were over, reach for her dressing gown.

"Untie it completely," he said, his hands at her small and warm waist. "And undo those buttons again, Priss. It is a new shirt and the infernal things are too small for sense and sharp at the edges, too. And then get back into bed. I don't know about you, but I'm tired. And there is no saying what I will be feeling after a sleep."

She smiled and pulled his neckcloth loose.

The barriers behind her eyes had all been lifted again, he saw when he looked into them.

7

She got to know him better after they had moved to the country, but she was not at all sure that she wished to do so. Her heart ached with the new knowledge and all the evidence it brought that he was a real person, with all the complexities and inconsistencies and pains and pleasures of a real man. It had been better, perhaps, to know him only as her employer, to know only his body with any degree of intimacy.

They arrived at Brookhurst early one evening, too tired to do anything but sink gratefully into baths, eat sparingly of a lavish meal that the cook had prepared in anticipation of their arrival, and retire to bed. He spent one hour in hers before retiring to his own.

But the next morning, though cloudy, was warm and inviting. Both had awoken to the loudness of silence and the chirping of birds and the distant barking of a dog. He took her outside after breakfast to show her the part of the park closest to the house.

"It is not a large estate," he said, drawing her arm through his. "We were never among the grand landholders of England. But it is large enough and the park has always been zealously preserved."

"It is lovely, Gerald," she said, closing her eyes for a moment and breathing in the warm smell of summer vegetation.

"The formal gardens are old-fashioned," he said, "but I would not have them changed after my father's death, although I had a head gardener who was bursting with progressive ideas."

"I'm glad," she said. "The colors and smells are glorious."

He led her to the side of the house, where there was a small rose arbor surrounded by trees. He led her through a trellised archway into an enchanted world of delicate blooms and heady perfumes.

"My mother's," he said. "It was her pride and joy."

"You have no family left?" she asked him. "Did she die long ago, Gerald?" She released his arm in order to cup a pink bud gently in her hands and breathe in its fragrance.

"She died when I was thirteen," he said.

He laughed. "I discovered that she was dead at the same time as I discovered that she had been alive."

She looked up at him inquiringly.

"My father told me she was dead when she left us," he said. "I was eight at the time. Priss, what mother would leave her son at so young an age, eh? I had thought she was fond of me, fool that I was. And then when I was thirteen he told me she was being brought home for burial, and we were both plunged into the farce of deep mourning, five whole years after I had suffered all of a child's grief at her loss. It seemed she had been living all the time with my aunts."

"I am so sorry," she said.

"Why?" he asked, looking at her coolly. "Were you responsible for anything that happened?"

She shook her head. "And you were an only child?" she asked.

"I was the one that escaped, so to speak," he said. "There were an alarming number of miscarriages and stillbirths, I gather. Something like six before me and four after me, though I may have the numbers wrong."

She closed her eyes. "Ah, poor lady," she said.

He shrugged. "It made it easier for her to abandon her responsibilities," he said. "She might have felt obliged to stay if there had been more of us, especially if there had been one still at her breast. One of those stillbirths happened only six months or so before she died the first time." He smiled and plucked a rose to weave into her hair. "You would think she would have loved the one child to live, wouldn't you?" he said.

"Oh, Gerald." She touched the lapels of his coat. "Are you sure she did not? Could an eight-year-old understand the complexities of what was going on in the adult world around him? Perhaps she had no choice but to leave you."

"Perhaps you are right," he said, turning away abruptly and striding out through the arch. "She was a woman, after all."

Priscilla went after him and walked silently beside him. He had his hands clasped behind his back. He did not offer his arm.

"You are the wise one, Priss," he said. "You know how to stop yourself from having children, stillborn or live. Whenever you wish to take yourself off, you can do so with a clear conscience, can't you? And in the process you will save a few poor mortals from imagining that there is such a thing as love in this world."

"Gerald," she whispered. And she was not sure if the intense pain she felt and the tears she fought were for the cruelty of his words or for the bleak disillusion that he had carried forward into his life from the age of thirteen.

He took his duties as landlord very seriously. She discovered that within just a few days of their arrival. He rode out almost every morning to visit his tenants and laborers, sometimes not arriving back until well after luncheon. And he talked about their problems and concerns and suggestions to his bailiff and sometimes to her, with furrowed brow. He usually stopped himself after a few minutes with her.

"But I must not bore you with man talk, Priss," he would say. "You must tell me to be quiet when I start prosing on."

"But I like to hear about your people, Gerald," she would say, and sometimes he would flash her a grateful smile and continue with what he had been saying.

Sometimes she longed to tell him that for years she had helped her father run an estate. She longed to talk with him, discuss matters with him, as well as merely listening. She longed to go with him on his visits.

But she held her peace. She did not want him to know her as she was beginning to know him. And of course it was out of the question for her to go anywhere with him that would bring them into communication with other people. She was his mistress and living with him, unchaperoned, at his country home. She imagined that gossip about her was rife in the neighborhood, with disapproval of his lack of taste in bringing her into the country with him.

He spent two whole days puzzling over the estate books in his study, a permanent frown on his face.

"Hazelwood explained it to me this morning," he said to Priscilla when she went quietly into the room during the afternoon and stood at his shoulder, looking down at the neat columns of figures. "But I never could make head nor tail of accounts. I'll understand them yet, though." He continued to frown down at the book.

Priscilla scanned it over his shoulder. He must have a very efficient bailiff. The accounts were clearly and carefully kept. They made perfect sense to her after five minutes. She could have explained them to Gerald. But she set one light hand on his head, her fingers playing with his hair, and stayed quiet.

"You don't need to be in here among all this man stuff, Priss," he said after a while, sitting up and circling her waist with one arm. "Why don't you put your bonnet on and go sit in the rose arbor? Am I neglecting you?"

"If you don't mind," she said, resisting only just in time the impulse to lean down to kiss his forehead, "I will fetch my embroidery, Gerald, and sit quietly in here with you. May I?"

He brightened. "Looking at your pretty face may inspire me with understanding," he said. "You don't know how fortunate you are, Priss, to be a woman and not to have such things to worry about."

"I know," she said. "I will leave the puzzling to you, Gerald."

It took him two days, but eventually he mastered all the business that had been conducted on his farms since his residence there the summer before.

Priscilla learned that he was restless and that frequently he did not sleep well. After that first night he told her that she might as well sleep in his bed at nights and save him the trouble of having to move from bed to bed. It was not an arrangement that she relished, giving as it did too much the illusion of closeness between them and foreboding as it did too much of loneliness for the future. But she had always obeyed him, even if on occasion she had argued with him. She obeyed this command without protest.

She became quite accustomed to waking in the night to find him tossing and turning beside her or gone from the room altogether. Once — it was early dawn — she got out of bed to look from the window and was in time to see him galloping off from the stables. Often when she woke he would be standing naked at the window, gazing out into the darkness.

Sometimes she left him alone with his own thoughts, knowing the importance of privacy. Sometimes she crossed the room to stand beside him, murmuring his name or leaving him to accept the comfort of her presence or ignore it as he wished.

On one occasion he set an arm about her and drew her against his side.

"You should be sleeping, Priss," he said. "Did I disturb you?"

"I am quite happy to be standing here with you," she said.

"Ah," he said, rubbing his cheek against the curls at the top of her head, "you are a good girl."

She kept him silent company until he began to talk.

"I should have sold it when my father died," he said. "It was foolish to keep it, was it not? There are nothing but ghosts here, anyway."

"Brookhurst?" she said. "You thought of selling it?"

"No, I didn't," he said. "That's the strange thing. Only now does it strike me that I should have done so. Sold it. Sold all the memories, all the ghosts. Let someone else live with them."

"Don't you love it, Gerald?" she asked. "I have had the impression that you do."

There was a long silence.

"I could never do anything right, you know," he said. "Never. I suppose it must have seemed a cruel fate to him that I was the one to survive when there were ten or so other possibilities. He told me once that most of those dead babies were boys. His sons. My brothers." He laughed softly. "But I was the one to live. God's joke on my father."

"Gerald," she said. "I am sure he loved you. You were his only son, his only child."

"I was never very bright, you know," he said. "My tutors used to despair of ever teaching me to read or figure. Figures especially have always been my demon. You wouldn't know, Priss, but there is so much to be learned and it always terrified me because I could not seem to make much progress."

"But I have seen you work through your estate books," she said, "and understand them."

"You would not realize this," he said, "and perhaps I should not tell you. Perhaps I should just let you continue to be impressed with my learning. But there are many who would have looked at those books and understood them in an hour. It took me two days."

"Gerald," she said, setting her head on his shoulder.

"He used to rage at me," he said, "until I got older and he realized it was hopeless. Then he was worse. He used to look at me with open contempt. Priss, you wouldn't know how I tried to please him, how I longed and longed to please him."

She lifted a hand and brushed a tear from her cheek.

"At school I scraped by," he said. "I would not even have gone to university if . . . Well, something happened to make me desperate to leave home. I went to Oxford and was a disaster there. It was all Greek to me, even the subjects that were not literally Greek."

"Gerald," she said, "it does not matter. Intelligence and knowledge do not make a man."

He laughed softly. "He used to rage at my clothes," he said. "I have to rely on my tailor and my valet to help me these days, Priss. I never know quite what should go with what. I can never quite see why it matters that something should match something else or that something should be all the crack. I didn't know that that blue dress of yours was unfashionable until you told me so. It's pretty. That is all I see."

She burrowed her head against his neck.

"My father was an educated man of culture and impeccable taste," he said. "And he was blessed with a son like me."

"I am sure that he loved you anyway, Gerald," she said.

"The only thing I was ever any good at was music," he said. "And I learned early that that was a feminine accomplishment and not in any way to be encouraged. A gentleman can be expected to appreciate good music and to be discriminating in his musical tastes, of course, but he must on no account be a performer."

She lifted her head. "You play an instrument?" she asked.

"The pianoforte," he said, shamefaced.

"There is one in the drawing room," she said with a smile. For days she had been aching to play it, and had even come close to giving in to the temptation when he was away from home. But she was afraid that one of the servants would tell him that she had been playing and there would be too many awkward questions for her to answer. "Will you play it for me one day, Gerald? Will you? Please?"

"I am out of practice," he said. "But I suppose I could play something for you, Priss, if you would like."

"I would like," she said. "Thank you."

He looked at her in the dim light that glowed through the window. He stroked one hand over her naked breast. "I am not sorry I brought you with me," he said. "You have a kind heart, Priss. I ought not to have said all these things to you. Now you will realize that I am a very ordinary man with many shortcomings. Certainly not hero material."

You are my hero, she wanted to tell him. But they were the wrong words to say. She was only his mistress. She searched for the right ones.

"You are a person, Gerald," she said, "no more and no less heroic than almost every other man you could name. You have always been good to me, and that is all I care about. The degree of kindness we show to other people is really all that matters, isn't it?"

"You are chilly," he said, drawing her close to his side again, "and you didn't even put anything on to keep yourself warm. Come. I have kept you from bed for too long. Will you mind if I keep you from sleep a little longer, Priss? I want you."

"You know," she said, "that it is always my pleasure to give you comfort."

"Not just your job?" he asked, settling her on the bed and cupping her face in his hands, smoothing his thumbs over her cheeks before joining her there.

"My pleasure," she said, reaching up her arms for him, opening her body to give him the treasure of her love, which he would recognize only as pleasure and comfort.

He got to know her better after they moved to the country, though he was not at all sure that he wished to do so. She began, little by little, to become a person before his eyes, a person with depths of character he had only guessed at before and accomplishments he had not dreamed of. It had been better, perhaps, to know her only as his mistress, to know only her body with any degree of intimacy.

She had very little to do with his servants, keeping away from them as much as she could and not even trying to interfere with the running of the house. And yet there was a quiet dignity about her, a ladylike demeanor, which appeared to win their respect within a few days of her arrival. They treated her with deference even though it must have been no secret in the house that she shared his bed at night.

She accepted without question the fact that when he visited his neighbors or accepted their invitations to some evening entertainment, he would go alone. And on the few occasions when visitors arrived at the house, she would take herself off quietly to some place where she would not be discovered without his having to tell her to do so.

It was after one such visit that he made a major discovery about her. He did not know where she had gone and had to ask his housekeeper. Miss Prissy was sitting in the conservatory, the woman told him. He went in search of her there.

It seemed she was unaware that the visitors had left. Or perhaps it was that she had not expected him to come looking for her. However it was, she looked up startled when he stepped close to her and hastily slid a book beneath the cushion of the seat next to her.

"Priss?" he said, frowning. "Were you

reading?"

"What?" she said. But she flushed. He had been far too close to have misunderstood what he had seen. "Yes, I was."

"You can read?" he said, withdrawing the book from its hiding place and seating himself beside her.

"Miss Blythe taught me," she said, her voice breathless. "It is just a little vanity, a little pleasure of mine."

"Journal of the Plague Year," he said, reading the gold writing on the spine of the book.

"By Daniel Defoe," she said. "I do not like it as well as *Robinson Crusoe,* though it is worth reading."

"I read that at school," he said. "*Robinson Crusoe,* that is. He is the one who got stranded on a desert island for so many years?"

"Yes," she said. "It is a marvelous depiction of how the human spirit can triumph over almost any adversity, even loneliness and near despair. And of how it can bring order out of chaos and something bearable and meaningful out of emptiness."

He frowned. "I found it a little tedious, if I recall," he said. "There weren't enough characters, though it started well enough with the shipwreck and all."

"Yes," she said, "I think you are right about the sparsity of characters, Gerald, though Friday is an interesting one."

"Kit taught you to read?" he said.

"Yes." She smiled a little uncertainly at him.

"How long were you with her, Priss?" he asked.

"Almost six months altogether," she said, "before you took me away from there."

"Six months," he said. "You must be an apt pupil."

She laughed and bit her lip. "But I had very little else to do," she said, and blushed.

He returned the book to her. "There are many volumes in the library here," he said. "My father collected them. You may go in there anytime you wish, Priss."

"Thank you," she said.

He found her in there one day when he was late returning from a lengthy discussion with one of his more garrulous tenants. She was sitting at the desk, writing.

"Gerald," she said, slipping the paper beneath the blotter and coming around the desk with her usual gesture of outstretched hands. "I did not hear you come. You must have ridden around to the stables by the other way. You have had a very long morning. I hope you have eaten. Are you very tired?"

"Only glad to be home," he said, squeezing her hands and stopping himself only just in time from leaning forward to kiss her cheek. "You write too, Priss? May I see?"

"Oh, it is nothing," she said hastily. "Only scribbles. A diary."

"Ah," he said, "a diary. Secrets. I won't pry, then."

"Thank you," she said. "May I bring you some refreshments, Gerald?"

"Come and walk in the garden," he said. "You will need your bonnet, though, Priss. It is hot out there."

He played the pianoforte for her the evening after admitting to her that he played. He took her into the drawing room, which he rarely used because of its excessive size, and seated her beside him on the bench.

"I am very out of practice," he said, "and never was exactly concert material anyway, Priss. Don't expect too much. My fingers would tie themselves together if I tried to tackle Bach or Mozart. I shall play you some folk songs. Perhaps you will recognize some of them. Did you ever hear music before you left home?"

"Sometimes," she said.

He played "Robin Adair" while she sat very still, watching his hands and listening. He was pleased to find that he made only two mistakes. It had been almost a year since he had last played. And he recalled that the previous summer he had spent hours of every day at the keyboard, killing the ghosts, thumbing his nose at his father's contempt for his feminine accomplishment, losing himself in the one form of beauty that could set his soul on fire.

He started to play "Barbara Allen." Priscilla hummed the tune quietly.

"You know it?" he asked.

"Yes." She sang the first verse as he played the melody again and continued on with the second verse. She had a soft and sweet soprano voice. The whole sad story lived itself out beneath his fingers and from her lips before they both fell silent.

"More of Kit's teaching?" he asked at last.

"I know the song," she said. "I heard it a long time ago."

"Priss," he said. But he said no more. He started to play a short Bach finger exercise, surprised to find that the stiffness was going from his fingers already. She had sung in a voice that had known some training.

Who was she? Devil take it, who was she? But he did not want to know. He was afraid to know. He wanted her to be Priss.

He was a little sorry for his decision to bring her into his bed all night and every night. But how could he order her back to her own bed without giving the impression that she had displeased him? He could never find the right words.

She was slowly banishing the loneliness and all the feelings of inadequacy that had haunted him all his life. She was there, always there. If he was awake and unable to sleep, and tossing and turning to find a comfortable position, she was there, quietly asleep beside him, a softness and a warmth to draw him. And he often moved closer to her, resting his head against her arm or wrapping his own carefully about her waist, and found that suddenly he was comfortable and sleepy again.

If he was too restless to lie on the bed and got up to stand by the window, he knew her to be sleeping quietly just behind him. He knew that when he was drowsy and ready for sleep again, he could climb back into bed and warm himself against her warmth and fall asleep in the circle of her peace.

And on those occasions when she woke up and came to stand beside him, he was able to verbalize in his mind, and sometimes out loud to her, what it was that was holding him from sleep, what it was that so very often held him from sleep. She pushed back the loneliness.

But he was sorry for it. For it was all illusion and there was the terror there constantly in the back of his mind that the loneliness, the emptiness, the futility, of his existence would rush back at him with even greater force when he was finally alone again — as he would inevitably be sooner or later.

She was a woman. Men did not pretend to give love. His father had never pretended. At least he had always known where he stood with his father. But women were the great pretenders, the dangerous ones. For there were men, gullible men like himself, who sometimes believed them.

His mother had always been there, too, to soothe away the loneliness of being an only child, to comfort him after a harsh word from his father. She had always been there. Always — until he was eight years old.

And Priss was always there now. Whenever he needed her, she was there. And it would be so easy to fall into the fatal error of believing that she would always, always be there for him. It was so easy even now to believe that she was there because she cared, because she wanted to be.

"You know that it is always my pleasure to give you comfort," she had told him on one occasion when he was feeling particularly vulnerable.

"Not just your job?" he had asked her, cupping her face in his hands and gazing down into her warmly smiling eyes before coming down on top of her.

"My pleasure," she had said.

And he had allowed himself to believe her for the rest of that night, burying himself in her soft warmth, imagining that it was love she gave, giving back love — though he had never learned how to please a woman — then lying on his side afterward, his arms about her, his head pillowed on her breast, her hand stroking lightly through his hair.

It had felt very good. Sometimes it was good to give in to such illusions.

Provided one remembered soon enough that it was illusion and not reality. Provided one remembered that she was being paid very well to create just such an illusion. Provided one recalled that even at Kit's whorehouse that very first time, when she had never set eyes on him before, she had smiled at him as if he were the only man in the world and pleasured him as if he were the only man ever to have possessed her.

Provided one remembered that she was a

woman. Just as his mother had been. And just as Helena had been.

Sometimes he wished that he had not brought her from London with him at all. And often he wished that he had left her in her own bedchamber, to be used only occasionally, when his body cried out for her.

8

They had been at Brookhurst for almost a month when the Earl of Severn arrived unannounced one afternoon.

"My mother and Connie have taken themselves off to spend a month or so with Pru and Theo and the children," he said, shaking his friend heartily by the hand. "I excused myself from accompanying them and came here on the chance that you would be in residence, Ger. You are going to entertain me for a couple of weeks." He grinned.

"I would have invited you," Sir Gerald said, "if I had thought you were going anywhere while still in mourning, Miles."

Priscilla was slipping quietly from the room. But the earl's voice stopped her when she had her hand on the doorknob.

"Prissy?" he said. "Did Gerald bring you down here, too?" He was walking toward her, his hand outstretched, she saw when she turned to look at him. "The country air must agree with you. You are looking remarkably pretty."

She looked at his hand, swallowed, and placed her own in it. "Thank you, my lord," she said, and would have continued on her way.

"You are not leaving on my account, are you?" he asked. "You must not do so. Ger, command your lady to stay, if you please. And where did you leave your manners this morning? My tongue is hanging out for a cup of tea."

"Nothing stronger?" Sir Gerald said. "Tea, Miles?"

"Tea in the presence of a lady," the earl said with a grin.

"Sit down, Priss," Sir Gerald said.

Lord Severn waited for her to sit before taking a chair himself.

She sat quietly with her hands folded in her lap while the two friends exchanged news and banter. And she gradually relaxed. He had made her feel like a lady again, the earl, just as he had when he had called on her in London with Gerald.

And he really was the most handsome man she had ever seen, she thought dispassionately. Doubtless every second female who looked at him fell hopelessly in love with him, and yet he seemed not to be a conceited man. She of course was not one of those females. There was no corner of her heart left to lose.

"Prissy," Lord Severn said, turning to smile at her, "we are being very ill-mannered talking of people you do not know. Connie is my younger sister, Pru my elder. Pru has two children already and is swearing to have five more before she settles into a dignified middle age. I am not at all sure I will have the energy to play uncle to seven energetic youngsters."

"But doubtless some of them will have grown to a quieter stage of maturity by the time all seven of them are out of the cradle, my lord," she said.

"Ah," he said, "the voice of sense. Is she always so grave and so wise, Ger?"

Sir Gerald smiled at her.

"Gerald," she said that night when she was undressing for bed, "I feel very embarrassed. I ought not to be here when the Earl of Severn is visiting you, but I do not know where I should go. Do you wish me to return to London?"

He frowned at her. "This is my home," he said, "and I have chosen to bring you here, Priss. Anyone who does not like it can stay away or take himself off as soon as he knows the truth of the matter. But you don't have to worry about Miles. He likes you."

"Does he?" she said. Certainly the earl had impeccably good manners. Whether or not he liked her she did not know. And even if he did, she supposed that he might find it distasteful to be staying at a home where the owner's mistress was in residence.

"I am wearing one of these infernal shirts again," Sir Gerald said irritably, "and I have dismissed my valet for the night. Come and open the buttons for me, Priss, will you?"

She crossed the room to him.

"There," she said a few moments later. "You just have to slip them through the buttonholes, Gerald, instead of tearing at them."

"That's easy enough for you to say," he said, smiling ruefully at her, "when you can manage to sew all those delicate stitches into your cloth. My fingers won't always do what I tell them to do."

"Yes, they will," she said. "On a keyboard they are faultless, Gerald. I will not hear you constantly belittling yourself."

He was laughing when she looked up into his face.

"Now I know how to draw a compliment from you," he said, pulling his shirt free of his waistband. "You sounded quite cross then, Priss."

"I *was* cross, too," she said, laughing back at him. "You are a very special person, Gerald, and do not even realize it."

"We had better go to bed," he said, "before my head swells too large to balance on my shoulders."

For a few days she succeeded in keeping out of the earl's way whenever Gerald was not with her. Yet when the three of them were together, he would invariably draw her into the conversation.

She was playing the pianoforte in the drawing room one morning when Gerald had ridden out on business as usual and Lord Severn had gone into the village. She had finally given in to the temptation to play a week or more before, having sat and listened to Gerald on several occasions. She hoped that the servants would never have occasion to mention the fact to their employer.

But when she finished a Haydn sonata that she had been practicing for several days, she jumped about on the bench, aware suddenly that someone was standing silently behind her.

"I startled you," the earl said with a smile. "I do beg your pardon. The French windows were unlatched and I was drawn by the sound of music. You have a fine touch."

She stood up, her heart pounding. "Please, my lord," she said, "don't tell Gerald."

His eyebrows rose. "He does not know?" he said.

"He plays himself," she said. "Very well."

"Yes, I know," he said. "That gives you something in common." He looked closely at her.

"He believes himself so lacking in accomplishments," she said. "But he has this, and I believe he is proud of it even though his father was contemptuous of his talent."

"Ah, yes," he said, "the late Sir Christian Stapleton. There was not one grain of humor in the whole man, I believe. You are afraid that you outclass Gerald, Prissy?"

"Oh, no," she said. "He is far more talented than I. But perhaps he would not realize that. Besides . . ."

"Besides being extremely kindhearted," he said, "you are a fraud and you do not wish Gerald to discover the fact."

She swallowed and took a hesitant step backward from him.

"You are the poet, too?" he asked.

"Poet?"

"There is a love poem — alas, incomplete — beneath the blotter in the library," he said. "I could not quite believe that even knowing you would have sent Gerald off into such flights of fancy, and the housekeeper seems rather too prosaic a soul to have tried her hand at anything of such sensibility. I thought it must be you, Prissy." He grinned at her, his blue eyes dancing, a dimple denting one cheek.

"Oh," she said.

"Did Gerald interrupt you before you finished?" he asked. "And you forgot to return for it? I do assure you it is quite safe. I would imagine that Gerald does not use the desk with any great frequency. And your secret is safe with me. Does he at least know that you are literate?"

"Yes," she said.

"Ah." He smiled again. "I *am* a very inquisitive fellow, Prissy. You will never know how much willpower I am going to have to use to do what I am about to do. I am about to turn around and stroll back out through the French windows. Do continue your playing if you wish. I shall come tearing back here if I should see Gerald riding over the horizon before he is expected."

He turned and suited action to words.

Priscilla did not sit down again at the pianoforte. She went racing off to the library in a veritable panic.

■ ■ ■ ■

They had been for a stroll, the three of them, along a grassy, shaded avenue lined with busts and urns, which the late Sir Christian Stapleton had brought back with him from his Grand Tour.

Priscilla had an arm linked through Sir Gerald's. She was feeling entirely happy. The weather was hot, without being oppressively so, and she had found the company congenial. They had done a great deal of laughing. She was feeling, she thought privately, quite like Priscilla Wentworth again.

"The devil!" Sir Gerald said as they came in sight of the house and saw a carriage drawn up before the front steps and three figures standing in a group on the terrace. "This is not the time of day for a social call, is it?"

It was well past teatime.

"It looks like a traveling carriage, Ger," Lord Severn said.

"It is, too," Sir Gerald said as they drew a little closer. "It's that ass Ramsay. He said he might call in on his way from Brighton to Bath. I'd hoped he would forget. That is Horvath with him. Who is the other? Do you know him?"

"Never seen him in my life," the earl said.

Priscilla tried to draw her arm free, but Sir Gerald clamped it to his side again.

"There's no need for you to take yourself off, Priss," he said. "You met Ramsay and Horvath at Vauxhall."

"I could slip into the conservatory, Gerald," she said.

Lord Severn took her free arm and drew it through his. "I can understand you wishing to avoid such a tedious encounter, Prissy," he said, "but we cannot allow you to escape when we have to endure it ourselves, can we, Ger? Smile, my dear. We are about to be sociable. Incidentally, my friend, I hope this is not how you and Prissy talked about me before I came within earshot on my arrival. What a lowering thought."

Sir Gerald snorted.

"We could not pass by, old chap," Bertie Ramsay said, clapping Sir Gerald on the shoulder after there had been a great deal of handshaking and laughter, "without stopping in to sample your hospitality. Could we, chaps? 'Stapleton is expecting me,' I told them, 'and will be disappointed if you don't come with me.' All the more the merrier when one is incarcerated in the country, after all, what? Ah, Prissy? You here, too? I just spotted you standing back there."

Priscilla inclined her head to him and Sir Gerald drew her arm through his again.

"You remember Prissy, Horvath," Mr. Ramsay said. "From Vauxhall? When I still had Lettie on the mount? Biddle, make Prissy's acquaintance. Stapleton's mistress. One of Kit's old girls."

"Perhaps we should step inside," Sir Gerald said. "You must all be ready for refreshments. It must be hot inside a carriage on a day like this."

"Keep your eyes to yourself, Biddle," Mr. Ramsay said with a roar of a laugh. "I have the first bid, old chap. I made a gentleman's agreement with Stapleton the last time I saw him — it was at Tattersall's, Stapleton, do you remember? — that I get the next shot at Prissy when he drops her. You remember that, Prissy girl. The next shot is mine. We'll see if I can plow a little deeper than old Gerald here." He winked.

Priscilla jerked her arm free and fled along the terrace.

"Now she has dashed off like a frightened rabbit, you idiot, Bertie," Mr. Horvath said as the three men turned to enter the house. "She wouldn't have you now if you could offer the Crown Jewels on top of twice what Stapleton pays her. Subtlety is what you need to woo a female, my boy. Subtlety."

"No," the Earl of Severn said quietly, laying a firm hand on his friend's arm. "Sorry to spoil your fun, Ger, but this one is all my pleasure. One broken nose or jaw guaranteed. Two or three if their owners don't button up their lips fast. Go to Prissy."

"I have a murder to commit first," Sir Gerald muttered between his teeth.

"Sorry," the earl said, "there will be nothing left for you to murder after I have finished with him. Go to Prissy."

Sir Gerald clenched his fists at his sides, glared once venomously at the unconscious backs of the three new arrivals, who were already disappearing inside his house together with the liquor they must have consumed in great quantities within the past hour or so, and strode off.

The Earl of Severn flexed his hands at his sides a few times and called after the three men.

"Ramsay," he said, "you'll not be going inside after all, I am afraid, my dear fellow. Something to do with contamination and fumigation, I understand. I fear I must be growing rather hard of hearing. Would you care to come closer and repeat what you just said concerning the lady who was standing here a few moments ago?"

"Oh, I say," Mr. Ramsay said, retracing his steps back down to the terrace and chuckling with amusement. "Prissy? A lady, Severn? That's a laugh, that is. Prissy was one of Kit's whores. Didn't you know? Half of London had her. She was always eager to spread . . ."

One moment later he was lying on his back, his jaw shattered, staring at the sky just as if it were full night and all the stars twinkling down at him.

"I say," Mr. Horvath protested, keeping his distance. "Not fair, old chap. You are one of Jackson's prodigies, ain't you? Handy with your fives and all that?"

"Do you have anything to add concerning Stapleton's lady?" the earl asked, looking steadily at him. "If so, step closer so that I will be sure to hear."

"I?" Mr. Horvath said. "I don't know the lady any more than I know Eve, Severn."

"And you?" The earl turned to the silent Mr. Biddle.

"Never heard of her until a few minutes ago," that gentleman said hastily. "Looked a perfect lady to me, though."

"Ah," the earl said. "Perhaps the two of you would be so kind as to assist your friend into your carriage. There is an excellent inn just two or three miles beyond the village, I have been told. It is well stocked with beverages, too, by all accounts. Or if you would prefer to travel farther toward your final destination tonight, I would estimate that there are still a few hours of daylight left."

He stood watching, his feet set apart, his hands clenched at his sides, until the carriage with its cargo of three foxed young dandies had rolled farther down the driveway.

"Priss."

Sir Gerald had found her at the small lily-covered lake among the trees, a beautiful part of the park that he rarely visited. She was at the end of the lake farthest from the arched stone bridge, lying facedown on the soft grass, her head on her arms.

"Priss?" He sat down cross-legged beside her and spread one hand over the back of her head.

"Give me a little time, Gerald," she said, her voice sounding unexpectedly normal. "I shall come back to the house in a little while. I just need some time alone."

He sat quietly beside her and kept his hand on her head.

"It was all my fault, Priss," he said. "I should have let you go to the conservatory. And I should have smashed his nose as soon as his eyes alighted on you. As it is, I had to leave that pleasure to Miles. He really will smash bones, too. He is a Corinthian, you know. I suppose you would have guessed. He has a splendid physique. But it should have been me to do it, for all that."

"It was no very dreadful thing," she said after another brief silence. "Only his language was rather coarse, and I found it humiliating to have those other men, and particularly Lord Severn, hear what he said. But he spoke only the truth. I am your mistress, Gerald. And I was one of Miss Blythe's girls."

He smoothed his hand over the back of her head. Her curls were warm from the heat of the sun.

"Gerald?" She turned over onto her back suddenly and looked up at him. "You did not really say that at Tattersall's, did you? You did not say — how did he phrase it? — that he would have the next shot at me when you grow tired of me? Please say you did not say it."

He closed his eyes and bent his head forward. "Priss," he said, "don't ask that. Don't you know me better than to ask that?"

She continued to gaze up at him.

"No," he said. "Why should you? I took you to Vauxhall with those men, did I not? I let you be in company with them and with that girl who thought all the vulgar talk and all of Ramsay's public pawing were funny. And I did it, I took you there, only so that another young lady would see me with you and stop setting her cap at me. But no, Priss, I did not say that at Tattersall's, though I did not pop Ramsay on the nose when he suggested it. I am sorry I did not. And I am sorry that I allowed this to happen today."

She did not answer him. And looking down into her eyes, he could see the traces of redness about them and on her cheeks. She had been crying. She had been deeply hurt.

"Priss," he said, touching the backs of two knuckles to her cheek and watching her widen her eyes in a vain attempt to prevent two tears from spilling over onto her cheeks.

She tried to smile at him and lost control of her facial muscles altogether.

"Priss," he said, leaning down and gathering her close into his arms. "Don't cry."

But those words only released the floodgates, as he might have expected. He knew nothing about giving comfort to a woman. He held her against him as she sobbed, rocking her against his chest, patting her back, feeling helpless and frustrated. He wished he knew how to give her comfort.

"Come," he said when she was finally quiet again. He fumbled in a pocket and drew out a handkerchief. "Let me dry your eyes, Priss. There, that's better. All the wetness gone. Here, take the handkerchief and blow your nose. That will clear out the nasal passages and make you feel better. Better now?"

She nodded and set the wet handkerchief down on the grass. She hung her head forward so that he would not see the redness of her face.

He wanted very badly to comfort her. He wished he knew how. He had always been so awkward about women. He lifted her chin with one hand.

"No," he said, when she grasped his wrist, "don't hide from me, Priss. It is just me. Just me."

He looked down at her mouth. He had never kissed a woman. It was a strange thought under the circumstances. But it was true. He had come close once, but he had never done it. He did not know how to do it.

He closed his eyes, lowered his head, and kissed her. And lifted his head again sharply. She was looking up at him, her eyes wide. She had felt sweet. Very sweet. Warm and soft. He could feel the heat of the sun on the back of his neck. He could hear the droning of innumerable invisible insects.

He touched her lips with his tongue before joining his own to them again, tracing their outline, pressing against the seam. She was very still in his arms. He could feel her lips trembling against his tongue, and then she opened her mouth and moaned as he thrust his tongue once inside.

"Priss."

He laid her back against the grass, struggling out of his coat, rolling it to make a soft pillow for her head. And he brought himself down half across her, cupping her chin with one hand, drawing down her lower lip with his thumb, plunging his tongue into her mouth, taking instant fire at the heat and moisture and softness he found there. She moaned again and sucked inward on his tongue.

He wanted to give her comfort. He wanted to give her pleasure. But he did not know how. He had only ever taken both from her, instructing her on the exact positioning and movement of her body that would give him the maximum pleasure.

He did not know how to love her.

He touched her with unpracticed hands, moving them over her, wanting her to feel good. He kissed her forehead, her cheeks, her eyes and temples, her chin and her ears. He kissed her mouth again, stroking into her with his tongue. She looked up at him with wide and wondering eyes when he knelt up beside her once more.

He drew loose the ribbon that held her dress tight beneath her breasts. And he lowered the dress down over her shoulders, her breasts, her hips, down her legs. Her undergarments and her stockings followed.

So familiar, the small and shapely little body. Except that her nipples were peaked and taut. He did not know how to . . . But yes, he did. Once he had been shown, though he had not wanted to do it at the time. . . .

He cupped her breasts in his hands, massaging them gently, rubbing his thumbs over the nipples, pressing lightly inward. Her eyes closed and her lips parted. He lowered his head and licked at one nipple and felt her shudder. He moved his mouth to the other breast.

"Priss," he said, and he moved his hands down over her hips and lowered his head to kiss her stomach. Her fingers twined in his hair.

He touched her with one hand in the warm, soft, moist place, where he knew her so intimately with another part of his body. He feathered his fingers over her, pushed two inside her, felt her muscles contract around them.

By sheer instinct he found a part of her with the ball of his thumb and pulsed against it with quick shallow movements. Her hips arched upward. When he lifted his head to look at her, it was to find that she had thrown her head back against his coat and opened her mouth in a silent cry of agony or ecstasy. He circled his thumb more gently against her.

He wanted to comfort her. He wanted to love her. But he had no experience and very little knowledge.

"Ah," she said, her hips lifting again, her hand grabbing for the arm that was working her. "Ahhh!"

"Priss," he whispered, watching her shudder out of control on the ground before him.

She turned her head to look into his face, her eyes deep with pain, wonder, bewilderment, pleading — he could not interpret the look. He had no experience.

He wanted to give her pleasure.

"You are still aching?" he asked her, bending his head toward her. "It is not finished?"

"Gerald." Her voice was a whisper. "Gerald."

He dragged off his Hessian boots and tossed them aside, fumbled with the buttons of his pantaloons and stripped them off. He tore at the buttons of his shirt.

"I'll make it better for you," he said. "Just tell me how to make it better."

But she said nothing as he put himself inside her body. She twined her legs about his, spread her hands over his hips to draw him inward to her, and drew him closer with inner muscles.

He set his jaw hard, held to her shoulders, and moved in her, alert to her every demand, waiting for her to take her own pleasure before he would allow his body to demand its own.

And yet somehow — and he knew instinctively that he should not allow himself to go too soon — they came together and cried out together. And they descended to a moist and panting peace together.

He rolled his weight off her, taking her with him, holding them joined, cradling her in his arms away from the hardness of the ground. And he kissed her openmouthed once more, even though he knew she was already asleep.

9

The Earl of Severn spoke to Sir Gerald alone two days after the incident with Mr. Ramsay and his friends.

"I'll be taking myself off home tomorrow, Ger," he said. "I must make sure that the place has not collapsed without me there to hold it together."

"Tomorrow?" Sir Gerald said. "You have been here only just over a week, Miles. I thought you were staying for at least two."

His friend grinned. "Ah," he said, "but I know when three is a crowd, Ger. I hate to be a poor sport."

Sir Gerald flushed. "It was just that she was upset with what that ass said," he said. "I have been trying to make it up to her, Miles, take her mind off it and all that."

"And doing extremely well by the look of it," Lord Severn said.

"You must not leave on that account," Sir Gerald said. "I would feel guilty, Miles. Priss is just my mistress when all is said and done."

"Well," the earl said, "the truth of the matter is, Ger, that I am mortally jealous and feeling my womanless state like a gnawing toothache. I am going to be in London the very minute my year of mourning is over and I am going to employ the most handsome, most voluptuous, and most expensive courtesan in town. I have the blunt and the consequence to do it with my new title. There are some advantages to being an earl, you know. And for a whole week, don't expect to find me outside my mistress's boudoir. For a whole week, Ger — day and night."

Sir Gerald laughed. "You will too, Miles," he said. "Remember that barmaid at Oxford? The redhead?"

"I believe that was only four days," the earl said. "She feared for her job if she stayed with me longer, if I remember correctly."

They laughed again.

"Of course," the earl said, sobering, "I am going to be dodging my mother and the girls once we are out of mourning. They are going to be in search of a leg-shackle for me. I can feel it in my bones. The very last thing I want is a leg-shackle. Not for another ten years or so, at least."

"Then you will have to say no," Sir Gerald said. "A firm no, Miles. You and I will remain bachelors together until our eightieth year, and by that time no one will want us."

"There speaks a man without female relatives," Lord Severn said. "I have the strange fear that I am not going to stand a chance."

"Then I pity you," Sir Gerald said, "and am grateful that I have no one in life to please but myself."

"Yes," his friend said, looking at him curiously from his very blue eyes, "there is that advantage to having a mistress rather than a wife, I suppose."

Sir Gerald was in his study with a tenant farmer who had arrived after breakfast agitated by some grievance. The Earl of Severn waited for his host to be free so that he could take his leave.

"Well, Prissy," he said, when she would have withdrawn quietly from the breakfast room, "you must take a stroll with me in the formal gardens, if you please. I have been meaning to get you to name all the individual flowers to me. Flowers are just flowers to me, I am afraid. But I am sure you know all their names and natures. Will you take my arm?"

She took it and smiled fleetingly up at him.

"I have been pleased to make your acquaintance in the past week or so," he said, leading her down the steps and across the terrace to the formal gardens. "Gerald is a fortunate man. And I must apologize again for what happened three days ago. It was very largely my fault since I would not let you escape. I should have noticed sooner than I did that all three of them were thoroughly foxed."

"It was Gerald who told me I was not to go to the conservatory, my lord," she said. "I always obey Gerald."

"Do you?" he said. "I envy him, Prissy. I wish I could find another such as you."

She darted a glance up at him.

"You worked at Kit's," he said. "For how long?"

"For four months," she said quietly.

"And have been with Gerald for almost as many more," he said. "You were very upset with what Ramsay said, Prissy, and I don't blame you. I am sure Gerald must have spoken with you on the matter and reassured you, but let me add my own assurances. You must not let yourself be dragged down by the vulgarity of a man far your inferior."

"Mr. Ramsay?" she said.

"The Honorable Mr. Ramsay, actually," he said. "Very far your inferior, Prissy. The words 'whore' and 'mistress' and all the other synonyms for them are only labels, you know. The person wearing those labels can sometimes transcend them. You do, very much so."

She swallowed. "Thank you," she said. "You are kind. But I am not easily crushed, my lord. When I entered into my profession, I did so deliberately and even with some pride. I know what I am. I also know who I am, and the two are not the same at all."

He smiled and patted her hand. "I have been to Kit's myself on a number of occasions," he said, "and only found an hour's entertainment. Gerald was more fortunate. Far more fortunate. He went there and found a very precious little jewel. I am glad to know that, Prissy — that who you are is so much more important than what you are."

"Gerald is waiting for you," she said. "And your carriage is coming from the stables."

"Ah," he said, looking back toward the terrace, "it is time for me to leave. No, you shall not slip your hand from my arm and melt into the background, Prissy. You shall come and say good-bye to me properly at Gerald's side. And do you realize that you have not named even one flower to me? I begin to suspect that you are no more knowledgeable about plants than I."

He shook Sir Gerald heartily by the hand a few minutes later, kissed Priscilla on the cheek when she would have curtsied to him, and was on his way.

There was a new wonder about the world and about life. A cautious wonder. A wonder because they had become lovers beside the lily-covered lake and had remained lovers ever since. Cautious because not a word of their new relationship had been spoken between them.

When she had woken up beside the lake, she had found herself lying on her side in his close embrace, the sun still warm on her naked flesh. He had been looking at her, not with a smile exactly, but with a look that had warmed her heart like a fire on a winter's night. She had gazed back into his eyes.

She never knew what he would have said. They had both started speaking together. When they had both stopped and smiled at each other, she had continued.

"It must be getting late," she had said.

"Yes." He had eased away from her and only then had she realized that they had still been joined. "Miles will be wondering where we are."

They had dressed in silence, not embarrassed because they were accustomed to each other's nakedness, but turned away from each other nevertheless. And they had begun the walk back to the house side by side. He had taken her hand in his after a while, lacing his fingers with hers, and they had looked at each other and smiled.

When they returned to the house, she had bathed the Earl of Severn's bruised knuckles despite his amused protests and rubbed ointment on them, and the three of them had conversed easily through dinner and for an hour afterward in the drawing room until the earl had excused himself, saying he needed an early night.

And they had gone to bed, too, and made love and slept and made love and slept all night long, saying nothing but commonplaces to each other. Their couplings had been shared and tumultuous. He had kissed her and touched her in ways that had made it impossible for her to lie still and passive as he had always liked her to be. He had lifted her right off her back once, bringing her over him, lowering her with firm hands on her hips, impaling her, and loving her until she had thought she must go mad with pleasure and pain.

The following day he had canceled his usual morning of business in order to walk with her in the woods toward the lake again and had strolled all about it with her, gazing at the lilies and the sun sparkling off the ripples caused by the breeze. They had stood on the bridge for a long time, looking across the lake, absorbing the warmth of the sun.

In the afternoon he had canceled half-made plans to return a visit to some of his neighbors and had taken her and the earl on a picnic instead.

The night had been like the night before except that they had tired faster and slept more.

But there had been not a word, except on topics that had nothing to do with anything. His eyes told her of wonders she dared not hope for, and his body took her beyond reality and caution into a world of love and security and forever. But he said nothing.

She could say nothing herself. She was a mere woman. Less. She was a fallen woman, his mistress, the woman he paid to provide him with sexual pleasure. It could be said that he was getting full value for his money during these days and nights. For undoubtedly, though they performed in ways that were not the ways he had always most liked, she was giving delight to his body.

He set an arm about her waist as the earl's carriage disappeared down the driveway, and drew her against his side.

"You like him, Priss?" he asked. "He has been a close friend ever since we were at university together."

"I like him," she said. "He's a gentleman."

"We were as unlike each other as it was possible to be," he said. "He was intelligent, always did well at his studies, was handsome, charming, popular with other students and with the g—. Well, with the girls. But he seemed genuinely to like me."

"There can be no doubt of that," she said.

He looked up to the sky. "This weather still has not broken," he said. "It's amazing. If I were like my farmers, I would say that we are going to suffer for this. But who cares? Let's enjoy it while we have it, shall we?"

"Yes," she said, smiling.

"I am supposed to join a party on a ride to Rosthern Castle this afternoon," he said. "I would be gone from luncheon to dinner. Shall I send my excuses and stay here instead, Priss?"

"It must be as you wish, Gerald," she said. "You must not stay on my account if you think you should go."

"But what if I should stay on my account?" he asked.

"Well, then," she said, smiling at him, "I suppose it would be all right."

"I still have not taken you up the hill, have I?" he asked, gesturing toward the back of the house, and the wooded hill that formed the northern boundary of the park. "It is a strenuous walk, Priss, but there is a splendid view from the top. Shall we do it?"

"Yes," she said. "That would be lovely."

"After luncheon," he said, turning toward the house with her, his arm still about her waist. "I shall have Cook make up a small picnic basket for us again. Come upstairs with me, Priss. I want you."

"Yes," she said as he hugged her closer.

The honeymoon lasted for two full weeks. The weather cooperated — there was scarcely a cloud in the sky during the daytime. The little rain they had was kind enough to fall at night. Her body cooperated — she had had her monthly period just prior to their first real loving. And the neighbors cooperated, leaving them alone, accepting, however disapprovingly, the fact that Sir Gerald Stapleton wished to spend his days with the unchaperoned young lady who was his companion.

Priscilla had always lived a great deal in her imagination. Perhaps that very fact helped her to distinguish between illusion and reality. She knew that what she was experiencing, what Gerald was experiencing, was not anything of any permanence. Men did not fall irrevocably in love with women they had taken from whorehouses. He would have too much pride to do so and would be too much a product of his society. And even if he wished to so thumb his nose at convention, society would not allow it. And society would inevitably win. It always did.

She had made her choice when she had taken her first client at Miss Blythe's and sacrificed her virginity to him. And she would not do anything as futile and foolish now as regret that decision. If she had not entered on her profession, she would never have met Gerald.

Things were as they were. For now, for this moment in time, however long it lasted — but it would not last very long — they were in love. She loved him beyond time, but even he — yes, it was not wishful thinking to believe so — even he was in love for this moment of time, though he said not a word to her of his feelings.

And they were lovers. Gloriously, passionately lovers. In all those encounters with so many different men at Miss Blythe's and in all her encounters with Gerald, she had never dreamed that the sexual act, which could be so distasteful and even ugly, could also be an experience of such beauty and — she could never find quite the right word. Goodness? It was a thing of goodness. With Gerald it was goodness. It was right. It was the way man and woman should be. The way *they* should be.

She gave herself up to an enjoyment of their honeymoon, knowing all the dangers of so relaxing her guard, knowing that honeymoons always end, that life intrudes again sooner or later. She could only hope that in their case it would be later.

It was two weeks after the Earl of Severn left. Two weeks and three days of love.

She recognized the exact moment when it came to an end. And she accepted it with a heart that immediately locked itself against hopelessness and despair. She had had her honeymoon, her two weeks and three days of heaven. Many women never knew as much in a lifetime.

She was at the lake, having walked there one morning while Gerald was out on unavoidable business with his bailiff. She was sitting on the low stone wall of the bridge, looking out across the water. She had not brought a book with her. She was content during those days merely to sit and dream when he was not with her.

She saw him coming through the trees, his step eager, a smile on his face. She felt her love well up inside her like a tangible thing, and returned his smile. When he came to the end of the bridge, she reached out her arms to him.

"I have been waiting here for you," she said. "I knew you would find me."

And he stopped. The smile on his face lost its animation and gradually died over the span of perhaps one minute, during which time he neither moved nor said a word. When he did speak, the honeymoon was over.

She knew it, and lowered her arms, and accepted it.

He was totally and quite consciously in love. He had always been in love with her, he supposed — with her small and softly feminine body, with her dark and shining curls and wholesome prettiness, with her eager, mobile face and warm smile, with her quiet good sense and practicality, with her unfailing good nature.

But he had never trusted her. She had been an experienced whore when he met her and had been trained by Kit Blythe, who had a reputation for being one of the best instructors in London, if not *the* best. It was Priss's profession to be all those things he had fallen in love with, her way of earning a living. And she had done well for herself. Life as his mistress was undoubtedly more luxurious and less demanding than life at Kit's.

Or perhaps it was himself he had never trusted. He had never in his life had a good relationship. Oh, there was his friendship with the Earl of Severn. But never a good love relationship. He had been incapable of inspiring love in his father, and his mother's love had not lasted beyond his infancy. Priss too, if he allowed himself to relax into his fondness for her, would let him down.

Of course she would let him down. He was merely the man who paid her salary.

He had always held her at arms' length, determined to take only physical comfort from her, and not even allowing himself to become dependent upon that. And he had always planned to let her go before it was too late for him. He had always thought of the end of his lease on the house in London as the time when he would settle with her and find his temporary comfort with other women.

Never with a mistress again. Never again.

But he had done something he had not tried to do in years, something he had been afraid to try. He had done it without conscious thought and without a consideration of his fear. He had reached out to her to comfort her, to give something instead of always taking. For the moment he had forgotten that the hand that reaches out to help always gets slapped aside. He had given to her.

And it was only after he had given there beside the lake that he realized what it was he had given. It was himself. And he realized that in giving he had received. He had received all the wonder of love, all the closeness to another human being that went far deeper than the mere sexual union of bodies and that did not depend at all on the medium of words.

He was deeply and consciously in love. And accepted her love for him — it was not all completely feigned; he would never believe that — and his for her as a gift.

And yet he said nothing to her. He did not need to — that was one reason why he said nothing. It was there between them, so obvious that even a third person could not miss it. Miles had had no intention of leaving quite as soon as he did. And Gerald did not know the words — that was another reason. He had never been good with words or swift with thoughts. There was no way of putting into words what was there in his heart and his head and his eyes and his body — and that he saw reflected in her.

There were no words. He did not try to find them. There were only the words of everyday conversation, which had nothing whatsoever to do with the communication that was all the time binding them together beyond the words.

"You should see it in autumn, Priss," he told her when he took her on the long trek over the lawns behind the house and through the trees and up the hill the afternoon after Lord Severn left. "A riot of color in all directions. I remember coming up here as a very small boy — I think it must have been with my mother — and twirling about and about to see all the reds and oranges and yellows blur into lines until I fell down."

She laughed with him and unlaced her fingers from his in order to spread on the grass the blanket she had carried beneath one arm.

"It is a lovely scene even in summer," she said. "Did you ever sled down the hill in winter, Gerald? Or is it too far from the house? I remember. . . ." But she turned to smile at him and did not tell him what she remembered.

"There was only me," he said. "I don't recall any children from the village coming out here in winter, though there were some tree-climbing sessions and torn breeches and spanked bottoms in summer."

She laughed again as he reclined on one elbow beside her and sucked on a blade of grass. And they both fell silent as she clasped her knees and gazed about her and he gazed at her. He made love to her before they opened the picnic basket, just as he had made love to her that morning before luncheon, and as he would make love to her all night except when sleep cheated them of pleasure.

He did not lose touch with reality during the two weeks that followed. He was in love and he basked in the glory of that love with his lover. But he knew that love never lasted. He had seen proof of the fact too many times with the people he had trusted and loved.

He knew that sooner or later he would realize with his heart as well as his head that

Priss was a totally ineligible lover. He knew that he would fall out of love with her just as surely as he had fallen in and that, when the time came, she would be merely his mistress again and perhaps not even that. He would make a settlement on her and go on his way while she moved on to another protector.

And he knew that she would fall out of love with him. There was no such thing as permanency of love with women, and Priss was not in the business of love, only in the business of giving the illusion of love.

He accepted the fact that what they had would not last. But he wanted it to last as long as possible and pushed back into his unconscious mind the certainty of the end.

And despite himself he started to trust her. He started to relax. He started to be happy.

He came upon her in the rose arbor one afternoon after enduring a brief visit from the son and daughter of his closest neighbor. She was reading.

"Ah," he said, "the loveliest corner of my whole property."

She set the book aside and smiled at him. "Yes," she said. "There is nothing more perfect than a rose, is there?"

He plucked a deep red bud, careful not to

prick his fingers, and threaded it into her hair, as he had done on a previous occasion.

"Yes, there is," he said, looking down into her eyes. "When I set them together, I can see that there is, Priss."

It was the closest he ever came to putting into words his feelings for her.

He leaned down and scooped her up into his arms and sat down with her. She smiled and nestled her head on his shoulder. When he looked down at her after a few silent, comfortable minutes, it was to find that she was asleep. They had been awake much of the night before.

He rested his cheek against her curls and closed his eyes. There was no gesture more touching than to fall asleep in another's arms, he thought. Just like a child. He felt trusted. And trusting, too.

Despite himself he began to trust her, to believe that perhaps after all he was worthy of being loved.

He wanted their idyll together to last forever. He knew it would not last that long, but he made plans to keep her there at Brookhurst, alone with him, away from the world, until it did end.

It ended two weeks and three days after it began. And it did not end gradually as he supposed he had expected it to happen. It ended in the span of perhaps a minute, perhaps less.

It ended, leaving him shattered and bewildered and unhappy and wanting only to get away from there and away from her. Away from himself.

10

Sir Gerald had completed his business with his bailiff. He had not rushed. He never did so when involved with duty. But he felt a rush of happiness when he was free again at last, and hurried to the house to find Priscilla. She was not in any of the daytime rooms or in the conservatory. Neither was she in the rose arbor, he found when he glanced in there. She would be at the lake. It seemed to be her favorite place.

She was there, he saw as he strode through the trees. The pink of her dress contrasted with the green of the trees and grass surrounding her. She was sitting on the wall of the bridge, her image reflected among the lily pads in the water below her.

He wanted to be with her. He wanted to touch her, to be enclosed in the magic that was her. He smiled when he knew she had seen him, and hurried toward her. She reached out her hands when he came to the end of the bridge in that gesture of welcome that had always been characteristic of her.

"I have been waiting here for you," she said. "I knew you would find me."

And something jarred in him. Some long-suppressed memory.

Helena. His stepmother. His father's second wife, whom his father had married exactly one year after the death of his first. She had been nineteen at the time, he fifty-four. Gerald had been fourteen.

Helena. So very much like Priss that he was dazzled now by the resemblance. Her hair had more reddish hues than Priss's and had been longer. She had been a little taller, perhaps, with a more generous figure. But so like Priss. Always happy, always warmly smiling, always generous with her time and attention.

She had been the one person in his father's life, Gerald had often thought, whom his father had loved. He had adored her, pampered her, lavished gifts on her. And she had always glowed in his presence, young though she was to have a husband so much older.

Gerald had still been hurting when the marriage took place, still bewildered by the realization that his mother had lived for five full years after he had thought her dead, still in misery over the knowledge that she had not loved him after all.

Helena had soothed the hurt and finally taken it away altogether. She had been a friend to him — an older, wiser friend who had brought the sunshine back into his life. She had always found the time to talk with him and to listen to all the pent-up frustrations and uncertainties and hopes and dreams of a growing boy. She had shielded him from his father's impatience with him. She had helped him with his studies, sitting patiently with him for hours while he memorized poetry and history, explaining with unending patience facts about numbers that eluded his understanding.

He had grown to love her dearly. Not as a man loves a woman, and not quite as a son loves a mother — she was, after all, only five years his senior. He had loved her as one friend loves another older and wiser friend. He had worshipped her.

She had always loved the outdoors and had laughed merrily whenever her husband had fondly accused her of doing so only because she knew she made such a pretty picture against the background of flowers and trees. She had had a habit of going up behind him, circling his shoulders with her arms, and kissing his cheek. Gerald had always marveled at how she could make so free with his grim father, and at how his father clearly liked it, though he rarely smiled.

Gerald often used to seek her out to share some confidence. He had sought her out one summer day when he was eighteen. The twenty-nine-year-old Sir Gerald could no longer remember what it was that had sent him hurrying so eagerly to find her. But he had known to seek her out at her favorite place — the lake.

She had been sitting on the wall of the bridge, wearing a low-cut pink dress, her image reflected among the lily pads in the water. As pretty as a picture. His father was quite right. Gerald had hastened his steps.

"I have been waiting for you," she had said. "I knew you would find me. So tell me all about it, Gerry." And she had smiled her warm smile and reached out her hands for his.

He could no longer remember what it was he was to have told her all about.

He had closed the gap between them and put his hands in hers. And he had talked eagerly on about something — he could no longer recall what. Poor foolish boy. She had had all his love, all his trust, there in her two hands.

"Gerry," she had said when he paused for breath, squeezing his hands, "you are all grown up, aren't you? And such a very handsome young man."

He had known that to be a bouncer. He had started to grin. But there had been something in her face.

"The young ladies must be turning their smiles and their wiles on you already," she had said. "Are they, Gerry?"

He had probably blushed.

"Ah, but you will need someone very special," she had said. "Is there anyone special?"

He had shaken his head.

"You are a virgin, Gerry?" she had asked in her soft, sweet voice.

Suddenly he had been aware of birds chirping, insects droning, silence.

"The first time should be beautiful for you," she had said. "It should be with someone who will know how to make it so."

She had smiled into his eyes and released one of his hands. With her free hand she had slid her dress off one shoulder and downward to expose a generous and creamy breast, its tip pink. And she had drawn his hand against it and beneath it to cup it. She had covered his hand with her own, guiding his thumb over her nipple, pressing inward on it with her own thumb over his. Then she had exposed her other breast in the same way and cupped it with his other hand.

He had stood still and terrified, the unfamiliar softness and weight of a woman's flesh in his hands, an uncomfortable heat surging through his body, a painful tightening in his breeches.

She had not taken her eyes from his face or stopped smiling.

"Does that feel good, Gerry?" she had asked. "You need not be afraid. Move your hands. Do what you will."

He had moved his hands over her breasts, looking down at them, swallowing awkwardly.

"Oh, Gerry," she said, her voice changed, husky, "you are so beautifully young. You do not know how I have longed to be touched by a young man. By you. You do not know how I have wanted you this summer."

She had reached out her hands and begun to unbutton his breeches.

He had turned in a panic and run.

A few weeks later, after two other such encounters, during one of which he had lingered longer and allowed her to fondle him, he had gone to his father and asked if he might go to university, though he had no capacity for learning.

Perhaps it had been the only time his father had been pleased with him. He had gone to Oxford very shortly afterward and lost his virginity to a thin and pockmarked chambermaid two days after his arrival there.

The only time he had seen Helena after that was at his father's funeral almost three years later. She had been heavily veiled in black and had never once looked directly into his eyes. She had taken the legacy her husband had left her and disappeared from her stepson's life.

It all flashed through Sir Gerald's mind as he stood at the end of the bridge again, looking again at a pretty, pink-clad, eagerly welcoming, warmly smiling woman whom he loved and whom he had begun to trust.

Just as he had trusted Helena with the fragile emotions of a boy whose mother had abandoned him and whose father was disappointed in him. He had learned with Helena — finally — that a woman's love is a fickle and a selfish thing. He had learned that the only person it was ever safe to trust was oneself.

And it was gone. All of it. Within the span of a minute or perhaps less. She was Priss, his mistress, the woman who satisfied him utterly in bed and made him comfortable out of bed. A paid employee, marvelously skilled at her profession. And he was the poor fool who could never quite seem to wake up to the realities of life.

She lowered her hands.

"It is getting a little chilly, don't you think?" he said.

She looked up at the sky. A small cloud had moved across the face of the sun. There were more clouds approaching.

"Yes," she said. "I think perhaps we are in for a change in the weather."

"We should walk back to the house," he said. "There are some letters and papers that need my attention."

"Yes," she said, getting to her feet, smiling at him.

"I have been neglecting them," he said, turning and clasping his hands at his back as she came down the arch of the bridge toward him and fell into step beside him. "I had better spend the afternoon in the study, Priss."

"Yes," she said. "I shall read. There are so many books in your library that I have not yet read."

They walked side by side in silence, not touching.

"I think we'll be going back to London

soon," he said. "Tomorrow, perhaps. Or better still, the next day. I have done everything that needs to be done here. The country gets dull after a while. It is time to go back. Will you have enough time to get ready?"

"Of course," she said. "It will be as you wish, Gerald."

"I think it is going to rain," he said.

"Yes." She looked up at the sky again.

"You ought not to have wandered so far from the house, Priss," he said. "You might have got caught out in it and taken a chill."

"But the weather is so warm," she said. "And it will not rain until later this afternoon, Gerald."

"Even so," he said. "You should not wander away, Priss, without letting me know where you are going. What if I had twice as much work as I do? I would have wasted precious minutes looking for you."

He could not believe the stupidity of his words or the irritability of his tone. It was almost as if the voice was quite divorced from his brain.

"I am sorry, Gerald," she said. "It will not happen again."

He spent the afternoon in his study, standing at the window watching the clouds move in, and sitting at his desk, his head in his hands.

What a prize idiot he had made of himself in the past two weeks, he thought — starry-eyed and lovesick over a whore. He thought of her as she had been at Kit's. He thought of all the other men who had possessed her there, calculated the numbers, wished he could put names and faces to them. He thought of the one who had smacked and bruised her face and deliberately visualized all the possible perversions the man had then subjected her to — and paid her for performing.

But, no. He rubbed his eyes with the heels of his hands. He was being unfair to Priss. It was not her fault that life was as it was and circumstances were as they were. It would be unfair to hate her and want to degrade her merely because she was doing well the job he had employed her to do.

And if she was a whore, then he was a man who found it necessary to employ whores because he was no good at real relationships.

He got to his feet and wandered to the window again. She had been right. It was still not raining, though it was going to do so.

"Priss," he said to her when they rose from the dinner table that evening after almost an hour of stilted conversation and loud silence, "I am going back to the study. There is still plenty to do, and I have made arrangements to leave the morning after tomorrow."

"Yes," she said.

"Don't wait up for me," he said. And he drew a deep breath and said what he had not thought he would have the courage to say. "In fact, you might as well sleep in your own room tonight. I won't disturb you then when I come to bed."

"As you wish, Gerald," she said.

"You might as well stay in there tomorrow night as well," he said, "and get plenty of rest ready for the journey. Journeys are always exhausting."

"If you wish," she said. "I shall say good night, then, Gerald."

"Good night, Priss," he said, glancing down at her mouth and turning to stride away in the direction of his study.

He spent the next four hours getting thoroughly and methodically drunk, the first time he had done so since the night in London when he had gone to her afterward. This time he kept away from her both for the rest of the night while his bedchamber spun around at too dizzying a pace to allow him to close his eyes and during the next morning when his headache felt as large as the house.

Priscilla relaxed against the cushions of the carriage and watched the scenery pass the windows. Soon — after two weary days — London would appear and she would be back home again.

Home! Yes, it was home, her workplace downstairs, the rooms in which her real identity lurked upstairs. She longed to be back there, back upstairs.

Gerald, she saw, turning her head from the window for a moment, was looking out the window opposite. Their shoulders almost touched, but did not quite do so.

"We will be there soon," he said, feeling her eyes on him. "We will both be home soon, Priss."

"Yes." She smiled at him.

"It will be good to be home," he said.

"Yes."

"The journey has been a long one." He reached out one hand, but before he could touch hers, he returned it to his knee. "You must be weary, Priss."

"Not too badly, Gerald," she said. "The carriage is comfortable."

All through the journey she had been making plans. He was tired of her. Their honeymoon had come to an abrupt end three days before. He had grown tired of her, as she had known he would sooner or later. She was not going to make a grand tragedy out of the situation despite the feeling of dull despair that gnawed at her consciousness. She would not let it in.

Soon, as soon as he decently could, he would break off with her, settle with her, and be on his way. Perhaps he would do it as soon as they arrived back in London, though she did not believe so. Gerald often found it difficult to be decisive. Perhaps he would continue with her for a few weeks or a few months. Perhaps until Christmas. Perhaps until the lease ran out on the house.

She wanted to end it herself. When one knew that an inevitable end was approaching, and emptiness and pain, it was sometimes better to do something to hasten that end, to feel that one had some small measure of control over one's destiny.

She should end it herself. She should tell him when they returned to her house that she no longer wanted to live there or be in his employ. She should tell him that she was eager to return to Miss Blythe's or to begin some other life.

Except that perhaps she was no more decisive than he. And the thought of returning to a life of whoring, of offering herself to more than one man each day and to any man who cared to pay for her favors, was nauseating and terrifying. It had not been so bad the first time because she had really not known what it would be like. She had not looked beyond that first terrible deflowering. Now she did know.

No, she could not go back. And yet if she left Gerald now she would probably have to. She had saved almost every penny of her earnings, and she had her diamond and emerald bracelet, but they would not be enough to keep her until the age of thirty.

If she stayed with Gerald, she could earn a little more money, another few months of freedom once she was finally alone. And if she waited for him to cast her off, she would be entitled to a larger settlement. Miss Blythe had arranged for that. If she was the one to leave him, the settlement would be small.

She wanted to end a relationship that had become nothing but pain. But real life forced her to be practical.

"I'll be leaving London again tomorrow," he said abruptly, and her heart turned over within her. "I have been promising to visit all sorts of people. I should call on my aunts. I must do it now without putting it off again as I have done so many times. I'll probably be away for a month or two."

"Early autumn," she said. "It will be a good time to travel, Gerald. Neither too hot nor too cold."

"Yes," he said.

The carriage was passing through some of the outer streets of London. They would be home soon.

"The lease on the house is good for a long time yet," he said. "I'll pay you three months' salary in advance, Priss, just in case I am away longer than I expect."

"Thank you," she said.

"You will be glad of the holiday," he said. "You have worked hard through the summer. I have been pleased with you."

She turned her head away to look sightlessly through the window. His voice was stiff, stilted. She guessed that he was feeling embarrassed, awkward. She did not believe that he had meant to be cruel.

But she could not imagine more cruel words. She had worked hard. He had been pleased. She would be in need of a holiday.

She waited for his coachman to put the steps down when the carriage stopped outside her house. She waited for Gerald to get out first and hand her down. Mr. Prendergast was already holding the door of the house open, she saw. Her housekeeper was standing beyond him, curtsying to Gerald, smiling at her.

Gerald stood in the hallway with her, surrounded by her trunks and bags, waiting for the servants to disappear.

"I'll be on my way, Priss," he said. "You will be glad of a rest, I imagine. You need not prepare to receive me tonight. I will be leaving as early in the morning as I can. I'll see you on my return."

"Yes," she said. She smiled at him, having to make a conscious effort to use the smile she had learned and practiced at Miss Blythe's, the one that came from deep behind her eyes. "Have a safe journey and pleasant visits, Gerald." She reached out her hands to him, not sure if she should do so or not.

He took her hands after looking down at them for a few moments. "You are a good girl, Priss," he said. "Take care of yourself."

"Yes." She hid far behind the practiced smile as he raised one hand to his lips and kissed it.

And he was gone. The hallway was empty except for her luggage. He was gone. For a month or perhaps two or even three. Probably forever. He would probably not come back, but would settle with her through someone else, his man of business perhaps.

She closed her eyes and tried to recall the details of the last time they had made love. A long, long time ago. Early in the morning three days before with the sun shining through the window of his bedchamber and the breeze flapping the curtains at the open window. An eternity ago.

He had touched no more than her hands in the past three days. And now he was gone.

"Mr. Prendergast," she called, "will you bring my things up, if you please?"

She smiled at him when he appeared at the end of the hallway and turned to climb the stairs with a straight back and a spring in her step.

Sir Gerald Stapleton left London a little more than a week after returning from the country, and stayed away for two months. He visited a cousin he had not seen since school days, a friend who had married and moved into the country to stay two years before, and the Earl of Severn. He called upon his aunts, his mother's sisters, only when he was ready to return to London and had almost decided that he would not go at all. The only time he could remember meeting them was during the week of his mother's funeral, and they had both ignored him on that occasion, almost as if his thirteen-year-old bewildered, hurt person had not existed.

Lord Severn, whose mother and younger sister were still from home, was surprised to see him.

"What, Ger?" he said, shaking him firmly by the hand on his arrival. "On your travels? But where is Prissy?"

"Priss?" Sir Gerald said. He had just spent a number of weeks trying, unsuccessfully, to keep her beyond the boundaries of his mind. "I could hardly bring her here, could I, Miles?"

His friend grinned. "I suppose not," he said. "It is very easy to forget that Prissy is not respectable. I am amazed that you have been able to tear yourself away from her. One could scarce see your head when I left Brookhurst, Ger, for the moon and stars clustered about it. And about hers, too, I might add."

"Nonsense," Sir Gerald said. "I just happened to be hot for her for a few days, that's all, Miles. She has a certain skill between the sheets, you know, that makes her quite irresistible at times — one of Kit's girls and all that. I have her back in London waiting to keep me warm through the winter. I don't think I'll keep her beyond the spring, though."

He hated the carelessness of his own words, their vulgarity, his disloyalty to the magic of those two weeks — and to Priss herself.

"Well," the earl said, "I'm sorry to hear it, Ger. I like Prissy. She is a real lady."

"Yes," Sir Gerald said. "She is a good advertisement for Kit's training, is she not? Could we talk about something else? I had my fill of Priss this summer. When are you planning to move to Severn Park?"

They did not talk about her again but spent a pleasant two weeks together, riding and hunting and fishing.

It was only at night that she haunted him. Even after two months he would wake and turn to her only to find the bed beside him empty and cold and his loins aching for a woman who was far away. And his arms aching. And his heart.

Perhaps, he thought sometimes, gazing out into darkness, perhaps it had not mattered. Perhaps it did not matter that everyone he had ever loved had rejected him. Perhaps it did not mean that no one ever could love him forever.

Perhaps Priss could.

But he did not want to risk it. He had come dangerously close during those two weeks to giving up all of himself, everything that was himself, to his love for her. Dangerously close. If he had done so, and if it had happened again, he did not think he would have been able to survive. He really did not think he would.

He was glad he had not risked it. He was better as he was.

She had not even been hurt or bewildered. She had not even asked him what was the matter, why he had changed. She had reverted immediately to the Priss she had been right from the start, right from his first meeting with her at Kit's.

If she had cried, pleaded, raged, anything — if she had only shown some emotion, perhaps things would have been different. Perhaps he would have risked it. Who knew?

But he was glad she had become the experienced mistress again. He was glad, though it had almost broken his heart, for the evidence she had given him that it had all been playacting for her, merely an act to suit what she had seen he had wanted for those weeks.

He was glad he had not risked the ultimate giving.

He wanted to be back with her. He ached for her. But the more he ached, the longer he forced himself to stay away. And he still did not know, when he finally decided to return, whether he would go to her again or whether he would send a servant to make the settlement with her.

Yes, he did know. He knew that all the way back he would persuade himself that he was going to break with her. And he knew that when he got back, then he would convince himself that it was only fair to tell her face-to-face that this was the end. And he knew that having seen her again, he would postpone the end.

Yes, he knew very well what he was going to do.

But first he would visit his aunts.

11

It was always amazing, Priscilla thought as October drew to an end and winter drew inevitably closer, how one always seemed to bounce back from adversity, how life went on when one thought that surely it must grind to a halt.

It had happened before. First when her mother had died when she was only ten years old, and it had seemed that the sun must have been snuffed out, too. And then again when her father had died and there had been the blow so soon after of Broderick's death. It had seemed that it would be impossible to recover from such a double blow, especially when she had discovered that no provision had been made for her except by her mother's will and that her cousin would only reluctantly provide her with even the minimum of care.

It had seemed that life could never again hold a moment of happiness when she had come to London and discovered the truth about the finishing school run by her old governess and when it had become clear to her that she would be able to get no employment except what she could find with Miss Blythe. She would not have been surprised if she had not survived her first client as one of Miss Blythe's girls.

And yet life had in store for her the greatest happiness of her life. It had sent her Gerald in the guise of a client.

For a while at the end of the summer it had seemed that life was too painful and too totally empty to be borne. And yet she had endured. In her upstairs rooms she had become Priscilla Wentworth again. She had resumed the writing of the book she had started in the spring, and she had painted the autumn she saw around her and a portrait of Gerald from memory. She had read and stitched and sung a little, choosing the songs he had played for her during the summer.

She did not try to put him from her mind. She did not try to fall out of love with him. She thought of him constantly and loved him and remembered their times together and waited patiently for the pain to go away and the less piercing ache of nostalgia to take its place.

She walked with Maud a great deal and visited Miss Blythe several times.

She did not expect Gerald to come back. She waited as time went on to receive word from him so that she could plan a more definite future. And as October drew to an end she started to look about her when she was from home, somewhat fearfully, hoping that she would never come face-to-face with him and perhaps see him happy with another woman. She hoped to be spared that, at least.

It was a surprise to her one morning, then, to receive a note in his own rather untidy handwriting, informing her that he would call on her that evening.

It was a formal little note. But he was to call himself? And during the evening? She stood very still, staring down at the letter. The evening?

She prepared for him and awaited him in the downstairs parlor for three hours that evening, not quite sure if she had made the right preparations, not sure how she should greet him — if he came.

He came very late. It lacked only an hour of midnight. She heard his knock at the door and his voice in the hallway. She stood up.

He was not drunk, as she half expected.

He was dressed formally, as if he had come from the theater or from a ball. His fair curls were rumpled from his hat.

She reached out her hands to him and smiled.

"Gerald," she said, "how lovely to see you again. Did you enjoy your visits?"

"Priss," he said, crossing the room to her in a few strides, taking her hands, and squeezing them until she almost winced. "Looking as pretty as ever. Yes, I did, thank you. Miles sends his regards. I got drawn into attending the theater with the Bendletons tonight. I'm sorry to be so late."

She smiled at him, disconcerted by his very direct gaze, uncertain of what her cue was. There was a short silence.

"How may I please you, Gerald?" she asked, and was dismayed to hear her words, the ones she had been trained to ask as soon as she had taken a gentleman into her bedchamber, with a smile to indicate that he might ask almost whatever he pleased, provided it did not go against the rules.

"It has been a long time," he said.

"Yes." She continued to smile. "Would you like to come into the bedchamber?"

"Yes," he said. He looked into her eyes again in that way that had her having to resist the urge to take a step backward.

"That is the reason I came."

Ah. So it was not quite the end, then. Unless he intended to do this first and then tell her. But still not quite the end. One more time, at least.

But it was as if those two weeks and three days had never been. She led the way into the inner room, closed the door behind him, turned for him to unbutton her dress, and stepped out of it — she had removed all her undergarments before coming downstairs earlier. She undid the buttons of his shirt and lay down on the bed on her back, watching him.

Just as if those weeks and days had never been.

He stood beside the bed for a few moments, gazing down at her so that she wanted to reach out and take him by the hand. *Put it into words,* she wanted to tell him. *I cannot read your eyes.* But she said nothing. It was not her place to speak.

"The usual, if you please, Priss," he said.

It was the only indication that there had ever been anything else between them. He had not had to give her instructions since she was at Miss Blythe's.

She smiled and opened her arms to him. "It will be as you wish, Gerald," she said. "Come, then, let me give you pleasure."

His body was so very familiar, slim and pleasingly well muscled, with the smell of a remembered cologne. She knew so well how to fit herself to him, how to tilt herself and yet remain relaxed so that he could reach deeply into her. She knew the slow thrust of his body, the developing rhythm, his long steady enjoyment of the act of love. She knew when to ease her hips from the bed so that his hands could slide beneath. She knew the final deep, firm penetrations, the warm gush of his seed deep within. She knew the almost soundless sigh against the side of her face.

He was so very familiar. Gerald. Her employer. The man who paid for the use of her body and for her tenderness. The man she loved.

Not her lover. Not her love. That Gerald had been different. That Gerald had not used her body. He had loved it. He had loved her. But that lover had gone and would never return.

Her employer remained. For the moment, at least. For the moment she held him warm and sleeping on her body. She hooked the bedclothes with one foot, grasped them with one hand, and pulled them up about his shoulders. She held them around him, an excuse to have her arms about him. And she memorized the feel of him, the smell of him, the quiet sound of his breathing.

He slept for half an hour. It was almost as if all the visits he had paid to Miss Blythe's had conditioned him to be done with his pleasure within an hour. He lifted himself away from her and the bed and began to dress.

"Thank you, Priss," he said when he was fully clothed again. She was sitting on the edge of the bed, wearing a dressing gown. "It was good. Your holiday is over, I'm afraid. I shall call again the evening after tomorrow."

"I shall be ready for you," she said.

"I'll try not to be so late," he said. "It was good of you to wait up, Priss."

It is my job, she almost said, but she stopped herself in time.

He was half out through the door when he stopped suddenly and turned to her. "Oh, here," he said, reaching into an inner pocket of his coat and drawing out a small package.

"What is it?"

He placed it in her hands. "Just a little gift," he said. "I bought it in York on my way home."

They were tiny diamond-and-emerald earrings.

"I thought they would match your bracelet," he said.

"Yes," she said, touching a finger to one of them. "Yes, they will."

"Well," he said, turning to the door again, "I must not keep you up any later. Good night, Priss."

"Gerald," she called after him. "Thank you. They are beautiful."

"Just a little something," he said, and continued on his way.

Priscilla held the earrings against her mouth and closed her eyes. She let the tears run unheeded over the back of her hand.

He had spent three days with his aunts, both unmarried, the younger ten years older than his mother. She had been their favorite, the apple of their eye.

"We were so very pleased for her when she married Sir Christian," Aunt Hester, the elder, explained to him when they had recovered from their surprise at seeing him and their stiffness with him. "He had property, you know, and a comfortable fortune. And he seemed a steady young man."

Yes, his father had been a steady man all his life.

"But all those babies," Aunt Margaret said with a sigh and a blush for his male presence. "And all but you dead at birth or even before, Gerald. Poor dear Doris."

"She worshipped you," Aunt Hester said. "You were all that had made her life meaningful, she used to say when she was lying upstairs dying. Did she not, Margaret?"

Aunt Margaret sighed again. "If you could but have brought yourself to write to her, Gerald," she said. "Just a few lines, dear. Just a line even. But there, boys are ever heedless, we used to tell her to console her. Did we not, Hester?"

"Write to her?" he said, leaning forward in his chair. "Write to her, Aunt, when I thought she was dead?"

Both of them stared blankly at him and exchanged looks with each other. And the whole truth came out. The whole simple truth, which he supposed both he and they should have guessed at years before.

There had been that time not long before his mother's "death" when she had been going to take him to visit his aunts. He was to stay very quiet about it, he remembered, so that it would be a surprise to everyone. He could remember thinking it great fun to steal from the house when it was still night, because even Papa must not share in the secret, and run without talking down the driveway to the waiting carriage. And great fun to ride all day in the carriage with his mother and put up at an inn for the night when it was too dark to continue on the road.

Yes, he remembered it when he really thought about it, though the memory was lodged so far back in his consciousness that he had not thought of it for years. And he could remember laughing merrily the following morning when he awoke to find his mother dressed and his father in their room. It had been a super game, but his father had been too clever for them. They all went home and he never was taken to visit his aunts. He could not remember being upset at the change of plans.

His mother, it seemed, had been thwarted in her plan to leave his father and to take him with her. And she had "died" just a month or two later. She had been sent away, banished, forbidden to see or communicate with her son ever again.

She had written, of course, sent numerous gifts, all of which had been returned to her.

"But we thought you might have written, Gerald," Aunt Hester said. "You had no quarrel with her, after all, and she said you had always been fond of her."

"Of course, dear," Aunt Margaret said, "we realized that perhaps your papa had forbidden you to write. But boys usually have a way of doing what they want to do despite their papas. And she was your mama."

"But I thought she was dead," he said. "Until her body arrived home five years later, I did not know she had been alive."

Aunt Hester dissolved into tears.

"Ah," Aunt Margaret said, "the cruelty of the man. I am sorry, Gerald, to speak so of your papa and him dead, too. But the cruelty. And she died so slowly, dear, of consumption." She held a handkerchief to her eyes for five full minutes.

"She will know," Aunt Hester said finally, straightening her spine and returning her own handkerchief to her pocket. "She will know the truth, Gerald. And there is no fear that your papa is where she is now to ruin her joy again. And she will be with your ten brothers and sisters, dear, and more happy than she ever was here, poor Doris."

They fussed around him, making a pot of tea and arranging several small currant cakes on a plate for him, respecting his need for silence.

And he sat silently, staring at the floor before his feet, grieving again for his mother who had died in loneliness, deprived of the one being who had made her life meaningful — him. He sat silently while his mother was restored to him again after sixteen bitter years.

And when he was able to think of the matter — later, after he had swallowed two of the cakes to please his aunts and drunk two cups of the overstrong tea, and after he had retired to bed, having refused their offer of hot bricks to set at his feet — then he was able to realize that he need no longer feel the burden of having failed his father.

His father had failed him.

He left his aunts three days later, much against their wishes and with many hugs and kisses to take with him. He was not allowed to leave before he had given a firm promise to return.

"Such a fine young man," Aunt Hester said. "And our own nephew, Margaret. Our only living relative apart from each other."

"And with poor Doris's hair," Aunt Margaret said. "Such lovely fair curls, Gerald, dear. And Doris's smile. And her good heart."

He made directly for London, though he did stop in York to choose a gift for Priss. He could scarcely wait to see her. He wanted to take her the world, and the sun, moon, and stars, too, for good measure. But instinct told him not to take her too lavish a gift. Something modest and personal would seem far more like the love offering he wanted it to be.

The earrings seemed to have been made for her. They seemed to have been made to match her bracelet. He drew them out of his pocket many times during his journey home to look at them and to dream of sitting beside her as she opened the package. He would take them from her hands and clip them to her ears himself, kissing each ear as he did so and then kissing her mouth.

He would tell her about his mother. He wanted her to know about his mother.

But one's nature does not change overnight, he discovered with some regret when he returned to London. It was all very well when he was far away to dream about what he would say and do. But he had never been good with words. He had never been easy in relationships with other people. And in the eleven years since his encounters with Helena, and the sixteen since the loss of his mother, and in all the years with his father, being suspicious of other people and unwilling to trust them with himself had become deeply ingrained.

And circumstances were against him. He dashed off a note to her the morning after his late return to town and then somehow got himself entangled in a misunderstanding that resulted in his having to escort Miss Rush to the theater with the Bendleton party. It was eleven o'clock by the time he got to Priscilla's house.

And why would any man visit his mistress at eleven o'clock? There could be only one possible reason. Clearly it was the reason she expected. She was the old Priss, Priss as she had been at Kit's and in his keeping until the summer had made her into his lover. She was a mistress waiting to be bedded by her employer.

Incredibly, foolishly, disastrously, he had doubted again. He had looked into her eyes for some sign, for some indication that the Priss who had loved him — surely she had loved him — really had existed and still did exist in the mistress who waited for him to take her to bed.

But she did and said only what her training had taught her to do and say. And that smile, which had always seemed so warm to him, was not warm at all, he saw when he looked searchingly into her eyes. It was not warm, and it was not a smile. It was a shield, a cold and metallic shield behind which she hid.

But who was hiding behind it? He was too uncertain of himself, too unwise in the ways of human nature, too innocent, perhaps, to dare to try to find out.

And so he allowed himself to fall into the ritual she began. He bedded her, and even told her before he joined her on the bed and mounted her that he wanted it the old way. He did not love her body at all. He used it for a pleasure that did not turn out to be pleasure but only physical satiety.

And he was punished justly. She was warm and soft and yielding — and utterly passive. The way he liked his women to be. Sex without a relationship. Physical intimacy without involvement. The illusion that he was in control, that he was master.

He left her at midnight and remembered his gift only just in time. He gave it to her not at all in the way he had planned. He gave it as if it were nothing to him, a mere bauble, an afterthought. And she received it accordingly. She looked at it, agreed that the earrings would match her bracelet, and thanked him — an afterthought.

Instead of spending the night with Priss, as he had eagerly planned to do since the day before, he spent it wandering about the streets of London again, telling himself that he had had a fortunate escape, that it was better so.

There had still, after all, been Helena. And

there was still his own nature, which was made for a dull and ordinary existence, not for love or passion.

He would make himself ridiculous if he tried to express his love. And the object of his love was not one who could be in any way fitted into the pattern of his life. Only as his mistress. She was his mistress already. He would keep her so for a while.

After a while he would have had enough of her. He would be glad to let her go, thankful that he had not said anything to her that would lead her to expect some permanent sort of relationship.

They settled back into the old way again. And really it was not so bad, each felt. Both were grateful that a crisis had been averted, an ending avoided.

He came, not during the evening two days after his first visit, but early in the afternoon, long before she was expecting him.

"The air is crisp, Priss," he said when she came running lightly downstairs, "and the sky blue, and all the leaves underfoot. I have come to take you walking."

"Oh, have you, Gerald?" she asked, her eyes shining at him. "Maud has a cold and I have not been able to go out since yesterday. I have been so cross. I almost dared all by venturing out alone."

"Don't even try it," he said. "You might feel the flat of my hand if I caught you at it, Priss."

But his tone was light, and she smiled at him. Not her practiced smile, but almost a grin. And he noticed that she was wearing her earrings, though they were not quite appropriate wear for daytime with a wool dress. Even he knew that.

They walked through Hyde Park, which was almost deserted at that hour of the day and that time of the year, crunching the leaves underfoot, swishing their feet through them.

"Just like a couple of schoolchildren," she said.

He told her about his mother. All of it. He had not planned to do so. Perhaps that was why the words came easily and fluently.

"Poor lady," she said when he had finished. "Some people know so little happiness in their lives, Gerald. I do not wonder that your aunt said what she did about heaven. One can only hope that there is a heaven, where the injustices of this life are set right."

"Yes," he said. "I wish I could have said just one word to her, Priss. I wish I could have said good-bye."

"Poor Gerald," she said. "But she was your mother. She knew your father and you. I think she would have realized the truth. Perhaps nothing as fiendish as your being told that she was dead. But she would have known that you did not stop loving her. Oh, she would have known that, Gerald."

He patted her hand. "Perhaps," he said. "You have a kind heart, Priss. Shall I take you somewhere for cakes?"

"There are cakes at home," she said, "and jam tarts."

"Let the jam tarts decide it, then," he said. "Home it will be."

He stayed with her until the following morning, and they were comfortable together the whole time with a quiet sort of friendship. He slept with his arm about her, her head on his shoulder, after coupling with her once. And he had slept the night through, he realized with some surprise when he woke up to daylight.

He kissed her hand when he was leaving and directed her to be ready for him in two days' time. He would take her to one of the galleries, he told her, and she should teach him how to be a discerning art critic.

"Oh, Gerald," she said, laughing, "there is no such person. There is only what you like and what you do not like."

"But I never seem to like the right things, Priss," he said with a smile. "I like what is pretty rather than what is considered great art."

She liked his smile when he was teasing. She wished he would relax and do more of it.

But she was content. The end was not quite yet, and she was glad of it.

And he planned how to please her. Now that he knew she was literate and intelligent, he planned to take her about to the places she would enjoy. No matter that he had avoided them during his years in London as he always avoided anything that would bring him only tedium. He would take Priss and enjoy seeing her happy.

"I shall see you the day after tomorrow, then," he said. He would not allow himself to see her more than once in every two or three days, he had decided during the night walk about London.

"I shall be ready," she said.

12

Sir Gerald's aunts invited him to spend Christmas with them, and he decided to go, drawn by the lure of family, which he had not known for years. It was not an easy decision to make. He wanted to stay in London with Priscilla.

But it was the best decision, he decided after it was made. If he stayed in town he would be besieged by the usual invitations from well-meaning acquaintances who pitied his lone state. And how could he reject such invitations, using as an excuse that he preferred to spend the holiday with his mistress?

Besides, he thought, Christmas was a time for love and intimacy. Perhaps if he stayed he would disturb the fragile peace and contentment that had existed between him and Priss since his return at the end of October. Perhaps love would flower between them again and leave them empty once more when the holiday was over. And perhaps this time they would be unable to pick up the pieces again. He did not want to lose her, he had discovered over the past two months.

"What will you do with yourself, Priss?" he asked her. "Will you be lonely?"

"No, of course I won't," she said to him, smiling. "Miss Blythe has invited me to spend the day with her. The girls have a holiday, you know, and will be feasting and celebrating. Perhaps I will call for an hour but not for the whole day. I shall stay here and celebrate with Mrs. Wilson and Mr. Prendergast and Maud. They have nowhere else to go. Miriam has asked me if she may have the afternoon free to visit her family. I have told her she must go on Christmas Eve and not return until the day after Christmas. The door will be barred against her, I have said, if she tries to return earlier."

"I suppose I will be gone for about two weeks," he said. "I wish I weren't going, Priss. I hate the thought of having two spinster aunts fuss over me for all that time."

"But just think of the pleasure you will be giving them, Gerald," she said. "You will probably come back fat from all the goose and mince pies they will have stuffed into you."

He grimaced as she laughed.

"Christmas is a wonderful time for families," she said. "I remember . . ." She stopped and smiled at him.

"Do you, Priss?" he said, running one knuckle along her jawline. "Shall we have Christmas before I go? I'll have a goose sent over for Mrs. Wilson to stuff and bring some holly. And we'll sing carols and all that sort of thing. Shall we?"

"That would be lovely, Gerald," she said.

And so they spent an hour the afternoon before he left for his aunts' decorating the parlor with holly, trailing ivy from the picture frames, arranging pine boughs on the tables. And he climbed onto a chair while she stood beneath him with raised arms as if to catch him if he fell, hanging a small sprig of mistletoe from the ceiling to one side of the door.

In the evening he returned, dressed in satin knee breeches and brocaded coat and elaborately tied neckcloth, just as if he were about to attend a ball at Carlton House. And she was dressed in a delicate gown of dark green silk, and wearing her bracelet and earrings.

"You look beautiful, Priss," he said, taking her hands and kissing her cheek. "The dress is new?"

"Yes," she said. "My big extravagance. You look very splendid, too."

"The shades of blue match?" he asked. "My valet assured me that they do."

"They do," she said, smiling.

They ate their Christmas dinner in the small dining room and then sat before the crackling log fire in the parlor, singing carols, vying with each other to remember the words to all the verses, laughing when they both fell silent in the middle of the fourth verse of "Good King Wenceslas."

"It goes on forever, anyway," he said. "It is a bit of a bore, if you want my frank opinion, Priss."

"Shall I read the Christmas story?" she asked.

"Do you have a Bible?" he said.

She fetched one from upstairs, always her treasured possession. She read the story while he watched her and listened.

"Priss," he said when she was finished, "Kit did not teach you to read, did she?"

"Yes, she did," she said quite truthfully. Miss Blythe had been her governess for eight years, from the time she was six.

"Just one year ago?" He frowned.

She smiled and closed the Bible and set it aside.

"I have a Christmas present for you," she

said. "I hope you will like it. I think you will."

"You shouldn't have, Priss," he said. "You don't need to be buying presents for me."

"I did not buy it," she said. "I made it." She got to her feet and drew a large flat package from behind a chair.

He untied the ribbon and spread back the wrapping paper. And found himself looking down at a watercolor painting of his house at Brookhurst.

"Priss?" he said, looking up at her in surprise. "You painted this? You paint?"

"I sketched it when we were there," she said, "and painted it here. Do you like it, Gerald? There are four of them."

He lifted away the top painting to find three others: the rose arbor, the grass alley, and the lake, the grass at one side dotted with daisies, the arched bridge at the other reflected in the water among the lily pads — the place where their love affair had begun and ended.

"Priss," he said, while she sat very still and looked anxiously into his face, "they are so very pretty." He looked up at her smiling ruefully. "Those are not very adequate words, are they?"

"They are praise indeed," she said, clasping her hands to her bosom in a gesture quite uncharacteristic of her. "You think them pretty, Gerald?"

"I am going to have them framed," he said, "and hung in the study at Brookhurst. Then when the account books make no sense to me, I will be able to look up and see them and enjoy them. Thank you, Priss."

He went out into the hallway to fetch two packages from the inner pocket of his cloak.

"For me?" she said. "Both of them?"

"One of them is foolish," he said.

She smiled down at him and opened the long package first. The necklace matched her bracelet and her earrings almost exactly.

"I have had to sit all through dinner," he said, "watching your bare neck and wanting to put this there, Priss. But I forced myself to wait. Let me clasp it for you."

"Gerald," she said, turning on the sofa they shared and bending her head forward, "you must have hunted forever to find just the right piece."

"I did actually," he said, turning her by the shoulders and examining his gift at her throat. "But it was worth it, Priss. It looks good and the set is complete."

"Thank you," she said. "I never thought to possess such lovely jewels again."

"Again?" he said.

She fingered the necklace and touched

one earring before answering. “I meant after you gave me the bracelet,” she said.

“Are you going to open the other package?” he asked. “You may think it foolish, Priss. You may find it dull. I am not sure of your tastes, but it seemed to me that you might like it.”

“Oh, I do,” she said a few moments later, gazing down at the book she had unwrapped. It was bound in brown leather with gold lettering and gold-edged pages. *“The Love Sonnets of William Shakespeare,”* she read, tracing the letters with her finger. “Oh, I do, Gerald. You cannot imagine. They are the most beautiful poems in the world.”

“Well,” he said, “I can remember reading that one about a summer’s day in school. I didn’t think it was half bad, actually.”

“ ‘Shall I compare thee to a summer’s day?’ ” she said quietly, opening her book to hear the pages crackle with newness.

“And then he twists it to make her seem lovelier than summer,” he said. “Rather clever, actually. He was a clever man, Shakespeare, wasn’t he, Priss? It is true too, isn’t it? Summer does not last.”

“No,” she said. “But it always comes again, Gerald.”

“Yes,” he said, struck by the thought. “I

suppose it does."

She lifted the book in order to smell the new leather.

"Well," he said, taking one of her hands in his, removing the book with the other and setting it on the sofa, "I am going to have to leave, Priss. I want to make an early start in the morning."

"Yes," she said, getting to her feet. "Don't be late, Gerald."

He had decided before coming that he would not take her into the bedchamber that evening. He wanted to have Christmas with her, even it if was eight days early. And he did not want her to feel that it was a work evening.

"One thing first, though," he said, leading her by the hand until she stood beneath the mistletoe. "Happy Christmas, Priss."

He drew her into his arms and kissed her for the first time since their love affair had ended in the summer, opening his mouth over hers as his lips touched hers.

"Happy Christmas, Gerald," she said, her arms up about his neck.

He kissed her again.

And he was glad he was not planning to stay and glad that he was not going to spend the whole Christmas holiday with her. For already, holding her in his arms, kissing her, resisting the urge to reach into her mouth with his tongue, he could feel the return of a deep tenderness that was not at all the same thing as the physical desire that had flared with their embrace.

"Have a safe journey," she whispered to him. "Be careful, Gerald."

"I'll be back with the new year," he said, putting her from him, picking up his gift from her. "I'll send you a note as soon as I am in town again, Priss."

"Yes," she said, one hand covering her necklace.

"Good night, then," he said.

"Good night, Gerald."

He leaned forward over the bulk of his package and kissed her again.

Christmas was not a pleasant time. Although she often and deliberately counted her blessings, Priscilla could not draw from the holiday any of the magic or joy that it had always brought with it until the year before.

He would be gone for only two weeks, she told herself. Not for an eternity. Not even for as long as he had been gone in the autumn, and she had lived through that. Besides, they had had a wonderful Christmas together before he left. And being without him was good practice. She must not — oh, she must not, she kept telling herself in some fright — become dependent upon him. He was her employer, not her lover.

She went to church on the evening of Christmas Eve, alone, in guilty defiance of Gerald, and sat unobtrusively at the back. It was the first time she had been to church since she had become a fallen woman. It was a beautiful service, and Christ was born as surely as he had been born every Christmas for more than eighteen hundred years, and all that was the Christ came into the world again. But it was something she observed rather than felt. She was an outsider.

She had never felt her exclusion from respectability so strongly or so bleakly. And when she was on her way out of church, a richly dressed lady glanced at her and drew her skirts against herself so that she would not brush against and be contaminated by the lone woman who could be nothing but a street prostitute.

She gave Mrs. Wilson and Mr. Prendergast and Maud their gifts on Christmas morning and sat with them to eat Christmas dinner. And she talked with them and laughed a great deal at Maud's incessant stories and Mrs. Wilson's scoldings at the girl for talking so boldly in the presence of Miss Prissy.

She visited Miss Blythe in the afternoon, taking with her an eager Maud, who liked the thought of a different kitchen with new ears to regale with her chatterings. The girls were all in high spirits at the holiday from work and the gifts that Miss Blythe had given each one. There was a carefully wrapped lace handkerchief for Priscilla, too. She stayed for two hours, extending the time she had planned to spend there for the sake of Maud — and for the sake of her own loneliness, too.

And she spent the evening alone in the upstairs rooms of her house, reading Gerald's book, as she had read it every evening since he had left, pausing over the one sonnet he remembered from his schooldays.

" 'And summer's lease hath all too short a date,' " she read, smiling rather sadly.

Yes, far too short. And summer would not come again, either, as she had told him it would. Not with Gerald, anyway. By the time summer returned, he would be only a memory to her and she to him.

She had been careless for a long time. She had known about it and worried about it vaguely. But not enough to do anything about it.

Oh, she never once neglected to cleanse and douche herself whenever he put his seed in her. She had always completed the time-consuming and tedious procedure that had been such a prominent part of her training and the part that Miss Blythe had always enforced most strictly.

But she had known — it had been stressed during her training — that speed was of great importance, that the seed must be flushed out before it had a chance to take root.

When she had shared Gerald's bed at Brookhurst, she had not got up after each coupling. She had been too embarrassed to do so, too afraid that he would question her. And during that two-week period of their honeymoon she had been too happy and too drowsy from their lovemaking to think about getting up from the bed in order to be practical.

By the time she did cleanse herself there, they had often been making love all night, and some of his seed had been in her for many hours. She had got away with it there. Her monthly periods had always come with relief-bringing regularity.

Yet now, ironically, when he did not often stay with her for a whole night, her carelessness had caught up with her. She was a week late. Only a week. But her cycle had always been perfectly regular. It had not been upset even when she first became sexually active. There was not a great deal of hope that she was wrong in her fears.

Besides, there was a deep, quite intangible physical certainty that she had taken his seed into her womb and had accepted it there. Part of him and part of her had united, and now there was a new life in her womb, a life that was both him and her and yet neither.

She knew that she had his child in her. Their child.

The realization paralyzed her with terror. There had not been a great deal at Miss Blythe's that could bring shame to any of the girls. Allowing oneself to be got with child was deeply shameful there, the one thing that would have even the most hardened of the girls hanging her head and quailing with terror at the scathing lecture she must face alone from Miss Blythe. Having to be sent away and looked after by Miss Blythe while awaiting the birth was slow and dreadful humiliation, the return to work and the pitying, wondering looks of the other girls an unenviable ordeal. Miss Blythe would not allow any girl who wished to remain with her to abort a child.

Priscilla did not have enough money — even if she sold her precious jewels — to keep even herself for the seven years until she could claim her mother's inheritance. She could certainly not keep herself and a child, too. And if she must work for her living, there was only one type of job she was qualified for, but Miss Blythe would never take her and a child, too. No abbess of any other whorehouse would take a child, either.

And if she were to take to the streets alone, who would look after the child while she was at work?

Yet she could not do — she would not do — what other girls always did. She would not give up Gerald's child. She would die before she gave it up.

She sat alone on Christmas evening, her book closed, one hand stroking absently over the smooth leather of its cover, opening her mind to the terror she had been repressing for a week. She was going to bear a bastard child, hers and Gerald's. And she would keep the child until death made it impossible for her to do so any longer.

But there were plans to make. She was going to have to bring her liaison with Gerald to an end within — how long? Two months? Three? Would it be very noticeable after three? Not outwardly, perhaps. But he frequently saw her naked. She would have to be gone within three months.

It would be as well. She had always lived with the conviction that when the lease ran out on the house he would also wish to terminate their agreement. And though he had seemed to be pleased and contented with her since his return in October, there had been none of the fire or the tenderness of that brief spell during the summer — except perhaps on the evening of their Christmas.

She was his mistress, one who satisfied him, one he was accustomed to and comfortable with. But still, when all was said and done, she was his mistress. And spring would bring with it a restlessness, a desire to move on to another woman, or to several women for a time, perhaps. Perhaps he would return to Miss Blythe's.

It would be as well to end her employment herself instead of waiting for the inevitable and humiliating dismissal. Perhaps since she would have been with him for almost a year and had always given him good and obedient service — perhaps he would overlook the fact that she was the one to end it. Perhaps he would pay her the full settlement he had agreed to with Miss Blythe.

Perhaps she would be able to demean herself enough to ask him. After all, she would be asking not for herself, but for his child, though he would not know it.

And perhaps she would go to Miss Blythe — almost certainly she would. She would endure the scolding that had never failed to dissolve into tears every poor girl who had ever had to face it. She would endure it because she also needed Miss Blythe's help. She had no idea what she would do after she had left this house and Gerald's protection.

Priscilla traced the gold lettering on her book, not seeing what she was doing. It was Christmas Day. She was thinking of another woman, who had given birth to a bastard child on that day. Mary, and her faithful Joseph, who had married her despite her disgrace, although he had not even been the child's father.

But then, of course, Mary had not been a whore.

"And then after church," Sir Gerald said, holding his mistress's naked body snugly against his side, rubbing his cheek against her soft curls, "they took me to a neighbor's house where it turned out every resident and his dog for a five-mile radius of the village was assembled. They had to present me to every mortal one of them, Priss. And every time I was their dear nephew and did I not resemble my poor dear mother to a quite remarkable degree? It was deuced embarrassing."

"But you must have given them so much pleasure, Gerald," she said.

"They just about burst with it," he said. "Aunt Hester knitted me an egg cozy large enough for my head, to be worn at night — complete with tassel. I tried to wear it to please her on Christmas night. I almost died of itch before midnight."

Priscilla chuckled.

"And Aunt Margaret knitted me a pair of mittens," he said, "in canary yellow. It was devilish embarrassing, I tell you, Priss, trotting along the village street on Christmas morning, an aunt on each arm, to take our constitutional, two canary paws waving in the wind for all to see and wince over."

"Gerald." She was shaking with laughter. "You are exaggerating."

"No, the devil I am not," he said indignantly. "I'll fetch them to show you, Priss, though I will not put the nightcap on my head to demonstrate. Maybe Prendergast could get some use out of it."

She chuckled again and fell silent.

He stretched his toes, feeling their warmth beneath the bedclothes and the warmth and relaxation of his whole body. It seemed to him that it was the first total contentment he had felt since kissing her good-bye beneath the mistletoe more than two weeks before.

He had intended to go home for the night after paying his visit to her, since he had an early appointment with his tailor the next morning. But he could just as easily go there straight from Priss's, he decided. He had not worn evening clothes. He yawned and settled himself for sleep.

"Gerald?" Her voice was a questioning whisper.

"Mm?" he said, trying not to lose the drowsiness that was settling over him.

"Gerald," she said, "when the lease runs out on the house, you will not be renewing it, will you?"

"Eh?" he said. "That's a few months in the future, Priss. I don't have to think of that yet. What put that into your head?"

"I thought a year would be long enough," she said. "I thought you would be ready for a change by then. You will, won't you?"

He was awake and irritable. What the devil?

"How would I know?" he said. "Don't worry about it, Priss. I will give you plenty of notice when the time comes. And I'll make a decent settlement on you. Go to sleep now."

"I think in the spring I should go home," she said.

"Eh?" he said. "Home? Where you came from, you mean?"

"They miss me," she said. "They want me to come back."

"They?"

There was a pause. "My parents," she said, "and my brothers and sisters. I am the eldest. I had to go away to work. But — but one of the boys is old enough now to work with Father and I can go home. I think perhaps I should, Gerald."

"Tell them I need you here," he said. "I won't hear of your going on a visit, Priss. Not for any length of time, anyway."

"I meant for always," she said. "They want me back for always. I think we are growing a little tired of each other anyway, aren't we?"

"I am not tired of you yet," he said, thoroughly angry and hurt — and with a cold thread of fear needling at his heart.

"And what you feel doesn't signify, does it, Priss? I don't pay you to be tired or anything else. I pay you to give me pleasure with your body."

It was always the way of human nature, one part of his mind told him, but not that part that controlled his speech. The best way to cope with pain was to pass it on to someone else. Be slapped and slap right back. Be hurt and hurt right back. He wanted to hurt her.

"Yes," she said.

"I don't want to hear any more about it, then," he said, his voice stern and implacable. Just like his father's. "You have a good enough job here, Priss, and I pay you well enough, too. And they don't really want you back. Not with the way you have been earning your living."

Her voice was higher pitched than usual when she spoke. "They do not mind," she said. "They say they do not mind. They love me for who I am."

"Then they can have you back later," he said, turning onto her, pushing her legs wide with his own, thrusting himself inside her, wanting to hurt her. "When I am finished with you, Priss. I am not finished yet. You can tell them that."

She turned her head to one side and

closed her eyes. She lay stiller than usual, unrelaxed, unyielding while he took her quickly, in anger and hurt and fear.

"I have to go," he said, drawing away from her as soon as he had finished. "I have an appointment with my tailor in the morning."

They were both silent as he dressed in the near darkness.

She was still lying on the bed, uncovered, when he turned to her before leaving.

"I'll be here in the evening the day after tomorrow, Priss," he said, so thoroughly his father that he felt fear at himself. "I'll expect you to be ready for me. And I don't want to hear any more of this nonsense. Understood?"

She looked blankly at him. "I shall be ready when you come, Gerald," she said.

He drew a deep breath and let it out slowly. He took a step closer to the bed in order to lay one knuckle against her cheek.

"Priss," he said, "why did you have to make me angry? And what do you mean about being tired of me? Haven't I treated you well?"

"Yes," she said.

"Have I ever neglected you?" he asked. "Or been brutal with you? Have I ever demanded too much of you or come to you too often?"

"No," she said. "You have always been good to me, Gerald."

"Well, then," he said, "why are you tired of me?"

She stared mutely up at him until he felt anger welling in him again. He clamped his teeth together and stared down at her.

"Well, then," he said. "I'm sorry. You will just have to treat it as a rather unpleasant job, Priss, which has to be done in order to earn your daily bread. I believe factory workers and coal miners must feel the same, though they have to toil for many more hours than you."

He turned and strode from the room.

"Gerald," she called after him in that thin, high-pitched voice that she had used earlier.

He did not answer her call.

13

Priscilla prepared herself with great care two evenings later, wearing the rose-pink gown he liked, and dabbing on some of the perfume she had indulged herself with on a shopping trip just after Christmas. She had washed her hair that afternoon and brushed it carefully into soft curls.

She had hurt him. She knew that. She had chosen just the wrong time to speak to him. She might have known not to speak of such things when he had been settling for sleep after making love to her. His mind had caught onto the idea that she had grown tired of him, and he was hurt.

She sat beside the fire in the parlor, her hands in her lap, planning how she would greet him, how she would smile, what she would say. She did not want him hurt. He had such a fragile sense of his own worth, anyway. She must convince him that she was not tired of him at all. She must find some other way within the next two months of leaving him.

She sat until one o'clock in the morning before taking one of the candles into the hallway and calling to Mr. Prendergast to lock up and see to the fire. And she lay awake upstairs for another few hours, alert for his coming.

The following two evenings followed the exact same pattern.

He came one week after his last visit, during the afternoon, when she was out walking with Maud. Mr. Prendergast informed her when she came in that he was awaiting her in the parlor.

And so after all she had to greet him with flattened hair and wind-reddened cheeks and nose and a mind unprepared for what she would say.

"Gerald," she said, rushing into the room. She hurried toward him, her hands outstretched. "I did not know you were coming. I am so sorry to have kept you waiting."

He kept his hands behind his back. "Hello, Priss," he said.

She lowered her hands and smiled at him a little uncertainly. "Shall I go and comb my hair?" she asked. "And get ready for you, Gerald? Are you willing to wait for a few minutes?"

"To go to bed?" he said. "I don't know, Priss. Is that what I want to do?"

She looked at him silently for a few moments. "You do not want it, Gerald?" she asked. "Tell me what I may do for you, then. How can I make you comfortable?"

"I don't know if you can," he said. "I thought it did not matter, Priss. It never mattered at Kit's. I paid for pleasure. It did not matter who the girl was or what she thought of me provided she did what she was directed to do. I thought it would not matter with you. You always did as you were told. You always knew how to please me. You still do. And I would wager that if I took you to bed you would give it me as I like it best. You would, wouldn't you?"

"I am here for your pleasure, Gerald," she said.

"Precisely," he said. "But the thing is, Priss, that you are not just any girl any longer. I suppose I have been with you too long. Maybe you are right about that. You aren't just any woman's body to me any longer. You are Priss. And I don't think I could derive any pleasure from being with you if you are tired of me. It should not matter because it is your profession and I pay you to do just that, don't I? But I can't do it any longer, that's all. So what do you want, Priss? Only promise me one thing. You won't go back to Kit's, will you? I don't want to think that any man who fancies an hour's sport will be able to have a go at you."

It was her chance. Her chance to end things with a fair degree of amity. It was her chance to draw maximum benefit from their separation, since he was the one suggesting an immediate breaking off of their relationship.

"Tell me what you want," he said. "I just can't bed you if the money is the only thing making you willing to do it, Priss. And don't come any closer. I don't want you touching me."

"Gerald," she said. "Oh, Gerald, I am not tired of you. It is just that — that they wanted me to go home and I thought I might as well if you were growing tired of me. I thought you surely would be after almost a year. And there was . . . There was the summer and — and the autumn. And I did not want to think that perhaps you did not know how to break it off with me."

She stopped talking and stared lamely at him. "I am not tired of you, Gerald. And it is not just the money. You were always my favorite, you know." She could feel herself flushing. "You were the only one with whom it was never — unpleasant. It has never been unpleasant with you. It is my profession and of course I had to do it before even when it was unpleasant. But it has never been so with you. Giving you pleasure has always given me pleasure too."

"Has it, Priss?" He looked at her wistfully. "I am not much of a man, am I? And I never learned how to please a woman. I don't . . ."

"I like you better than any other man I have known, Gerald," she said. "And you please me well enough."

"Even last summer?" he said. "You were not disgusted, Priss? I did not work you too hard?"

"It was not work." She whispered the words, hurt now herself. "You know it was not work, Gerald. You know it."

He smiled a little uncertainly. "I think it was the summer, Priss," he said, "and the warm weather and the rustic surroundings."

"Yes," she said.

He reached out one hand to her and she placed one of hers in it. "You will tell them that you have a job you do not wish to leave, then?" he asked.

She nodded.

He drew a deep breath and let it out. "Let's go into the next room, then, shall we?" he said. "No, Priss. I don't care that your hair has been messed by your bonnet. It looks good enough to me. And I don't care that you have clothes on under that dress. You can remove them next door. Come with me? Now?"

Fool, she thought as he led her by the hand into the bedchamber and closed the door. *Fool, fool, fool.* She was one month with child already. A practiced eye, a less innocent eye than Gerald's, would perhaps already see the beginnings of change in her breasts. She would have to be away from him within the next two months.

And yet she had just declared her love for him, in so many words. She had just allowed him to begin a new and indefinite phase of their relationship.

Fool, she thought as he undressed her with his own hands and as she undressed him. She was allowing him to make love to her again. It was not going to be the usual coupling. It was going to be love. His hands were already at her waist, arching her into his body. His tongue was already stroking into her mouth. She was already responding.

Ah, Gerald, Gerald.

"You were very close to your family, Priss?" he asked her much later, holding her in his arms, against the relaxed warmth of his body.

"Yes," she said.

"It must have been hard for them to see you go," he said, "and hard for you to leave."

"Yes."

"Did you know when you left," he asked, "what you would do?"

"No," she said. "I suppose women never do. They always assume, I suppose, that there will be a respectable position available. I don't believe any woman enters this profession from choice, Gerald. At least I have never known any such woman. All the girls at Miss Blythe's simply had nothing else of value to sell."

"Your family must have been upset," he said.

"Yes."

"But they must love you very much," he said, "to tell you that it makes no difference to them. They must love you to want you back anyway, Priss."

"Yes," she said.

"I am going to send you on a visit to them," he said. "In the spring, Priss. For a month. Perhaps two. No, not two. For six weeks at the longest. I'll send you when spring comes." His fingers were stroking gently through her curls.

"Thank you," she said. "Thank you, Gerald."

"I want you to be happy," he said. "It will make you happy, Priss?"

"Yes," she said.

"Well, then," he said, "you must go. I'll arrange for it."

He was sleeping five minutes later.

Priscilla closed her eyes and breathed in the warm masculine smell of his cologne. The back of her throat and her chest ached and ached.

The Earl of Severn came back to town early in February and took up residence in his house in Grosvenor Square. He had left off his mourning and was ready to do some living, he told his friend.

They went to the opera together one evening, but Sir Gerald ended up walking home alone afterward while the earl made his way to the green room. Three days later, when Lord Severn finally arrived again at his friend's door, bathed and clean-shaven and dressed in fresh clothes, but with shadowed, somewhat bloodshot eyes, it was to announce that he had set up a new mistress.

Jenny Gibb, dancer, had the reputation of never looking lower than a duke and fifty thousand a year for a protector. She could afford to be particular since there was very little argument over the claim that she was the most beautiful, most curvaceous, and most fascinating creature to grace the capital in a decade.

Of course, Sir Gerald thought, pouring both of them a brandy, Miles was probably her male counterpart, bloodshot eyes and general sleepless appearance notwithstanding.

"I thought you said it was going to be at least a week," he said, handing the earl a glass.

"Ah, Ger," his friend said, "it would have been, too, with any ordinary woman. But the fair Jenny is no ordinary woman. Far from it. I am going to need a two-hour workout at Jackson's every morning to stay fit enough for her. Not one wink of sleep, Ger. Not one. And strenuous acrobatics every minute of the time. Three nights and two days of it."

"You aren't boasting, by any chance?" Sir Gerald asked.

"I?" the earl said. "Boasting? You forget I have a year's energy and frustrations to work off. How is Prissy? Are you still with her?"

"Still with her," Sir Gerald said. "I am going to send her into the country next month or the month after to visit her family. They wanted her to move home, but she decided to stay for a while longer."

"Ah," the earl said, "true love is winning its way, is it, Ger?"

Sir Gerald frowned. "That's nonsense talk, Miles," he said. "Priss is my mistress and deuced good at her job, too. Not like Jenny or anything like that, but then I don't look for anything like that."

"No," the earl said with a smile, "I could have guessed that Prissy is not anything like Jenny, Ger. But then Prissy is a lady. Jenny is not, for which blessing I shall be eternally thankful. Any decent cattle at Tattersall's these days?"

"You want to look?" Sir Gerald asked. "I'll come with you for an hour. I have promised to take Priss to the British Museum later on."

The earl laughed. "Culture with your mistress?" he said. "A strange combination. Perhaps an erotic combination? Are you going to show her the Elgin marbles?"

Sir Gerald flushed. "I most certainly am not," he said. "I am not having Priss gazing at a lot of naked men."

The earl threw back his head and laughed. "Did Priss not work at Kit's once upon a time?" he said.

Sir Gerald put a glass down and got to his feet. "Are we going to Tattersall's or are we not?" he asked. "I think we had better, Miles, before I end up popping you one on the chin and getting myself knocked senseless as a result."

Lord Severn looked levelly at him. "Sorry, old chap," he said. "That was not too tasteful a remark, was it? If I may, I'll drop by Prissy's with you and pay my respects before you bear her off on the culture hunt. I take it the visit is for Prissy's benefit rather than yours?"

"She has a way of explaining things," Sir Gerald said. "If she had been one of my teachers at school, Miles, I think perhaps I would have understood a few things. I might even have turned out to be a scholar."

The earl clapped a hand on his shoulder. "Today's food for thought," he said. "Get me out into the air, Ger, will you? I still have Jen's perfume in my nostrils even though I almost scrubbed my skin off just three hours ago."

She could not wait any longer, Priscilla thought, staring into the darkness. Not even another week. She had already waited far too long. It was the end of March. If she did not have the type of figure that did not show pregnancy early, she would not have been able to wait even this long. And almost any man but Gerald would surely have noticed long before.

She had delayed and delayed, constantly stealing just one more day and just one more day. Their relationship had entered a new phase of quiet tenderness since January. The passion of the previous summer had not returned, except during some of their lovemaking, but the dispassionate, almost purely sexual relationship of the autumn and early winter had passed, too. There had been a tenderness, a closeness, almost like that she imagined existing between a man and his wife in a good marriage once the honeymoon phase of their relationship had passed.

And because of her carelessness she had to destroy it all, both for him and for herself.

His arms were about her from behind. She was lying facing away from him, her head cradled on his arm, her body resting warmly against his. She must end it the next time he called. She must speak to him as soon as he arrived. She had her story all ready. It was just to have the courage to use it.

"Mm," he said, waking and rubbing his cheek against the top of her head, kissing her just above her ear. He shifted position a little, spread one hand over her stomach.

She closed her eyes, memorizing the moment, wishing she could suspend time. Why did one have to move on into the future? Why could one not choose to remain in an eternal present?

"Priss," he said, moving his hand over her, "too many cream cakes. Or perhaps it is the jam tarts."

She froze.

"I am going to have to talk to Mrs. Wilson," he said, "and get her to starve you for a few weeks."

She kept her eyes tightly closed. He kissed her above the ear again.

"I'm teasing," he said, his voice amused. "You are not taking this as a scold, are you, Priss? I don't mind if you put on a little more weight. You are just a little bit of a thing, anyway." He ran his hand again over the soft beginnings of swelling. "You feel good."

She set her hand over the back of his and laced her fingers with his.

"Gerald," she said after he had fallen silent again.

"That voice," he said warily. "I know something serious is coming when you speak like that. Have I hurt you? I didn't mean to, Priss. You always look pretty to me."

"No," she said, "I am not hurt."

"What, then?"

"I have had another letter from home," she said. "It was not from my parents this time. It was from a — a friend. A man friend. We were going to be married before I came here."

His arms were still about her.

"He was unable to support me," she said. "But he has his own cottage now and regular work. He wants me to come home, Gerald."

"To stay?" he asked.

"To stay."

"He knows about you?" he asked.

"Yes," she said. "He says it does not matter. He wants me to go home and marry him."

There was a lengthy silence.

"What do you want to do?" he asked.

"I think perhaps I should," she said. "I used to be fond of him."

"Used to be," he said. "You are not now?"

"It is an opportunity that will not come again," she said. "It is not that I have grown tired of you, Gerald, or want to leave you. You have been good to me. But girls like me do not usually have the chance to marry and have homes of their own and perhaps child—" She swallowed convulsively. "And perhaps children!"

"No," he said. "I suppose they don't."

There was another long silence.

"You are going, then?" he asked.

"I think perhaps I ought," she said.

"Priss," he said, "what is he like? Is he likely to throw any of this in your face at some time in the future? You should not do it if there is any chance he will start calling you a wh—. You should not do it if it is ever going to be humiliating for you."

"No," she said. "He is not like that, Gerald. He still loves me, and he blames himself for what has happened to me. He wants to make it up to me."

"And you love him too, Priss?" he asked.

She closed her eyes so tightly that she could see lights behind them. "No," she said. "But I was fond of him and think I can be fond of him again. It is not that I want to leave you, Gerald, but I have the chance to be married and respectable again."

"I think you should go, then, Priss," he said. "I really think you should."

"It is not quite decided yet," she said. "I have to reply to his letter and wait for him to send for me. But I think I might."

"Yes," he said. "You would be foolish not to."

"Yes."

He lay behind her for quite a while longer, holding her against him with both arms.

"I had better go, Priss," he said at last. "It does not seem right to be holding another man's woman. I had better go."

She pressed her cheek against his arm. "It is not that I am tired of you, Gerald," she said, "or that I wish to leave you. If this had not happened, I would have been content to be your mistress for as long as you wanted me. Perhaps I still can. Perhaps he will not write back."

"Well," he said, easing his arm from beneath her and sitting up at the side of the bed, "if he does, I think you should go, Priss, provided you really want to and provided you are sure he will not cut up nasty at some future time. I really think you should. I'll be glad to know that you are well settled."

"Will you, Gerald?" she asked.

"Yes," he said. "I have never liked the thought of your going back to Kit's when we finally break up, Priss. You know that. You have a lot to give to one man. You were not made for a whorehouse."

She did not turn off her side. She lay faced

away from him as he dressed.

He set a hand on her shoulder as he was leaving. "Good night, Priss," he said. "I'll call the day after tomorrow. Just to see if you have decided anything definite. Perhaps I will take you for a walk if the weather is good."

"Yes," she said. "I'll be ready, Gerald."

"Not for bed, though, Priss," he said. "Just for a walk."

"Just for a walk," she said.

He squeezed her shoulder and left.

If this was despair, she thought, closing her eyes, not moving, setting her hand over her slowly rounding womb, then it was hell enough. Hell could be no worse.

Sir Gerald had had a great deal on his mind even before going to his mistress's house. He had been in a bad mood, something she had detected and soothed away within half an hour of greeting him in her parlor. She had restored him to good humor in her usual quiet, sensible way.

"It cannot be as bad as you think," she had said. "I will not believe it of Lord Severn. He would not do anything quite so cynical, Gerald. Or if he did, he would make the very best of it afterward. I know he will. You will see that I am right."

"I suppose so," he had said, frowning. "But it is for a lifetime, Priss. Too long a time even if he knew the woman. A lifetime is always too long a time. Marriage was something dreamed up by a sadist, believe me. But he does not know the girl and chose her quite deliberately because she is plain and mute and dull."

"First impressions are often deceiving," she had said. "You have a headache, Gerald? Let me fetch some lavender water and soothe it away for you."

He had not had a headache, but he had not said so. He had allowed her to take his head in her lap and bathe his temples with lavender water and smile down at him. He had allowed her to baby him and make him sigh with contentment and feel again that life was good even if Miles was a chucklehead.

The earl had come back to his rooms with him from White's the evening before, gloomy because his mother and his sisters were on their way to town for the Season, as was the young lady they had chosen for his bride, and her family.

"If you could set before me the plainest, dullest, most ordinary female in London," he had said, "or in England for that matter,

I would make her an offer without further ado."

Sir Gerald had laughed at him. "It would be better to be like me, Miles," he had said, "and just tell the world in no uncertain terms that you will remain a bachelor as long as you please, and that will be for a lifetime, thank you kindly."

Sir Gerald had not taken his friend seriously despite his continued gloom.

"My ideal woman," the earl had said a while later, "is someone who would be nice and quiet, who would be content to live somewhere in the country and be visited once or twice a year. Someone who would make all the matchmaking mamas, including my own, fold up their tents and go home. Someone who would fade into the background of my life. Someone I could forget was there. Does that sound like bliss?"

"Better still to have no one, even in the background," Sir Gerald had said.

"That seems not to be an option." The Earl of Severn had got to his feet. "I should be going. It must be fiendishly late. I had better go to Jenny and enjoy myself while I still can."

He had not taken his friend seriously, Sir Gerald thought. It was all very well to talk in such a way. Acting was another matter.

But he had met his friend earlier that day at Jackson's and left with him to walk to White's. It seemed that the earl had met his dull, ordinary woman when she had come to his house that morning to beg his help in finding employment, pleading a distant relationship. He had promptly offered her employment — as his countess.

"You have done what?" Sir Gerald had asked, almost causing a collision with a lady and gentleman walking behind them when he had stopped abruptly on the pavement. But his ears had not deceived him.

"I have offered marriage to an impoverished relative who called on me this morning," the Earl of Severn had repeated. "Miss Abigail Gardiner."

They were to be married by special license in two days' time. And that reminded him, Sir Gerald thought, stumbling home from his mistress's house, his mind a bewildered blur of thoughts he did not feel inclined to sort through for the moment, that he would not be able to take Priss walking in two days' time. He had promised to be best man at Miles's wedding.

The world had gone mad.

And Priss was going to leave him. But he refused to look at the yawning emptiness that he knew would be there waiting for him when she was gone. It was not even certain yet that she would go. Perhaps her country swain would change his mind when he realized that she was willing to accept his offer.

Anyway, he would think of her leaving when she left.

He went straight to bed, burrowed his head far beneath the blankets, and waited out the remainder of a sleepless night.

14

Priscilla had not been to visit Miss Blythe for several weeks. She had felt too sure that her former governess and employer would see the truth, and she had not yet steeled herself to asking for the help she knew she would need. She went the morning after her talk with Gerald.

"Priscilla, my dear," Miss Blythe said, removing her spectacles from the end of her nose and closing her book, "how lovely. I have been wondering if you had fled the country. Do have a seat. I was relaxing for a few minutes after spending an hour with a new trainee. I am not at all sure that the girl will do. Her vulgarity is very deeply ingrained."

"I have not known you to fail yet," Priscilla said with a smile, kissing the offered cheek before seating herself.

Miss Blythe's eyes passed over her. "I have been wondering why you had not called," she said. "Now I can see the reason."

"It is so obvious?" Priscilla asked.

"To a trained eye," Miss Blythe said. "Your face is rounder, Priscilla, and your breasts fuller. How far along are you?"

"Close to four months," Priscilla said.

"You are one of the fortunate ones, then," Miss Blythe said. "Some women swell like balloons after only a month or two. Does Sir Gerald know?"

"No."

"And how do you explain its happening?" Miss Blythe asked, seating herself in her favorite chair again.

"I was careless," Priscilla said.

"Despite your training?" the other asked. "I suppose you thought you could take your ease all night beside your employer and not have to bear the consequences. I suppose you forgot that you are always at work and never at pleasure when lying with a man, Priscilla. It was one of the first facts you learned."

"Yes," Priscilla said. "I was careless."

"I suppose," Miss Blythe said, "you forgot that you are a person only when not with a client or employer, that with him you are an object. You forgot that objects are without emotions and must be carefully looked after if they are to be kept in order. You forgot,

have seen with my own eyes that she is settled and content. I don't intend to make trouble, if that is what you fear. I'll not make myself known to any of her family or acquaintances there. I just want to see her. If she is happy, I will leave immediately. If she is not, then I will bring her back with me. She was not unhappy with me, I flatter myself enough to believe."

"Sir Gerald," Miss Blythe said, "do you think you are being quite fair to Prissy? Do you not think it would be distressing to her to see you, to be reminded of what she is trying to put behind her?"

He stared at her for a long time. "Then I will stay out of her sight," he said. "I will merely make inquiries about her from a distance, perhaps see her without being seen. If I can see that she is contented, then I will leave. You have my word on it, ma'am."

She looked at him consideringly.

"I am fond of her," he said. "I will not do anything to hurt her. I want her happiness. I have grown fond of her."

"Very well, then," she said briskly, seeming to have come to some decision. "She came from the village of Denbridge in Wiltshire, Sir Gerald. I believe you will find some word of her there."

His shoulders sagged with relief. He had

not really expected that she would give him the information he had asked for. Dealing with Kit Blythe had always reminded him rather of dealing with the Rock of Gibraltar.

"Thank you," he said. "Thank you, ma'am. I will not do anything to make her unhappy, I promise you. I want only her happiness. Priss deserves happiness."

"Yes," she said. "Unfortunately, Sir Gerald, people rarely get what they deserve in this life. Perhaps that is why we have had to invent a heaven."

It was the only hint of cynicism he had ever heard from Kit Blythe, the only hint of humanity.

And why had he wrung that information from her with such passionate determination? he asked himself as he walked away from the house. He lifted one hand to his face and wrinkled his nose. The girl had been wearing perfume. Priss had almost never worn perfume. She had smelled of clean and wholesome soap. And when she had bought herself some perfume after Christmas, it had had a soft musky scent. Priss had always had impeccable good taste.

Was he really going to go down there — to Denbridge in Wiltshire? Was he? Was he going to so demean himself as to run after a former mistress just like a lovesick puppy? Could he not accept that good-bye meant good-bye?

But she had made her decision so hastily, he told himself, and she had made it somewhat reluctantly, deciding on marriage, he thought, only because she had felt that it was the right decision to make. She had wanted to stay with him. He was almost sure of it. She had sobbed her heart out in his arms when they were saying good-bye.

It was only right to see that she was happy with her decision now that she had met the man again, and to bring her back if she was not. He owed her that.

He would leave the next day, he decided. He had obligations, but he would see to freeing himself from them in the morning. In the afternoon he would set out on his way. He was not going to think anymore. He was just going to do. Once he had seen her and found her contented or even married already, then he would be able to return to town and get back to living again. He would be able finally to put her out of his mind.

He asked for Lady Severn on Grosvenor Square the following morning. But she was from home. It was the earl who came to speak with him.

"I asked her for a set at Warchester's ball tomorrow night, Miles," Sir Gerald explained, "but I shall have to excuse myself, I'm afraid. I'll be out of town. I'm leaving this afternoon, as a matter of fact."

The earl raised his eyebrows.

"Priss has probably been to the altar and back already and settled down to cozy domestic bliss," Sir Gerald said. It was what he had been telling himself all night. "But I am going down there to see, anyway. Perhaps if I offer her a raise in salary and buy her a few more jewels, she will come back. Do you think?"

He did not at all need his friend's opinion. He knew the answer. Priss would come back if she was unhappy — perhaps. She would come back if she was fond of him — perhaps. She would not come back for money or jewels. Not Priss. It was the most foolish idea he had had in a lifetime of foolishness.

"Is that what you want?" the earl asked. "I thought you were feeling a little tied down, being with the same woman for a year."

Sir Gerald felt uncomfortable. He shrugged. "I was comfortable with her," he said. "She suited me. She knows how to please me. The damned woman I had at Kit's last night wanted to tell me what I wanted, but it was not it at all."

"You haven't thought of marrying her yourself?" the earl asked.

"Eh?" Sir Gerald looked at him in surprise. Miles suggesting such a thing? It was the one thing his own mind had not even touched upon. Marry his mistress? "Marry Priss? My mistress? Good Lord, Miles, she was one of Kit's girls for a few months before I set her up. She was a whore." He whipped himself with the word, with the conviction that his friend's suggestion was totally preposterous.

"Why do I get the impression," the earl said, looking keenly at him, "that you would flatten the nose of anyone else who used that word to describe her, Ger? You are on your way, then?"

"Yes." Sir Gerald ran one hand through his fair curls. He had that feeling again that he was about to cry. He really should be whipped for using that word to describe Priss. Not Priss. Priss had worked for a living in the only way available to her. She had never been a whore. She was his comfort, his friend, his lover. His lo—. Yes, she was, or had been. Yes she was. She was his love. "I'm on my way."

She was his love. That was what she was. She was his love.

He did not leave for Wiltshire that afternoon after all, though he told no one that he was still in town. It was almost a week before he left, after running about almost constantly on business that seemed quite impossible for a while, and was frustrating every moment of the time.

But finally he was on his way, chafing at the delay and the greater certainty it brought that Priss would have been married in the meanwhile.

16

It was incredible, Sir Gerald thought as he neared the village of Denbridge in Wiltshire and decided to put up at the Cock and Pheasant Inn a few miles away. He must be even more incredibly stupid than he realized. He did not know Priss's last name.

She had been with him for almost a year. He thought of her as a friend and even his love. And yet he knew her only as Priss. He winced at the realization of the extent of his attitude of superiority over her, at the way he must have looked down upon her all the time, thought of her as a woman of no particular account. How could one know a woman so intimately for a year and yet know only her first name?

It hampered his inquiries. He was able to find no trace of her in his walks about the village or on his rides in the surrounding countryside. He was as discreet as he knew how to be, and yet eventually, sitting in the village tavern with a pint of ale on the table before him, he had to ask if anyone knew of a Prissy, who had worked in the kitchen of his sister's house in London, and whom his sister had begged him to ask after on his way west. No one knew any Prissy. Certainly not one who had recently returned home from London.

"There is Bess," one young man suggested with furrowed brow. "Bessie, some calls her. It sounds a bit like Prissy, don't it now?"

"Bessie has never been farther than five miles away in all her born days," someone else said with scorn.

"Both her parents are still alive," Sir Gerald said. "And several younger brothers and sisters." She had left his sister's service in order to return home to marry, he went on to explain. And no, his sister had neglected to furnish him with the girl's last name — a foolish oversight.

The men gathered at the tavern looked collectively thoughtful and collectively shook their heads. No, this Prissy was not from their village.

"There was Miss Wentworth from the house, of course," the same young man who had suggested Bessie said. "She were Miss Priscilla Wentworth, weren't she, before she took herself off from here when his worship and lordship decided to come down here and be king and duke and bishop and lord mayor all rolled into one?"

The man who had treated the young man scornfully before did so again. He clucked his tongue. "The gent is talking of a wench that worked in a kitchen, Ned," he said. "Keep your trap shut if you can't get no sense to come out of it."

The youth retired into an injured silence.

The rector later confirmed what Sir Gerald already knew in his heart. Denbridge was not Priss's home. Miss Blythe had misled him or Priss had misled her.

He did, before he returned to London, draw his horse to a halt outside the gates of Denton Manor and gaze along the straight driveway to the neat early Georgian manor, which was the home of Mr. Oswald Wentworth, he had learned. Miss Priscilla Wentworth, daughter of the late owner, and cousin of the present one, no longer lived there.

But he did not pursue his search at the house. It would be too ridiculous.

Except, he thought on his return journey, that she could read and write and the evidence was that she must have learned both skills longer ago than just the year before. And she could sketch and paint in watercolors and embroider. And she sang with a trained voice. Her accent had never once slipped into anything less than refined, even when she had been in an emotional state. And her manners and good taste were impeccable.

Miles had called her a real lady. So had Bertie Ramsay.

Her parents had written to her, she had said. The man she was to marry had written to her. Devil take it, was he quite stupid? This family and this swain, whom he had imagined to be poor and illiterate laborers, had *written* to her?

Good Lord!

Miss Priscilla Wentworth.

But it could not be. If he had been incredibly foolish all along with Priss, he was in danger now of outdoing his own stupidity. It could not be. Miss Priscilla Wentworth had not returned to Denton Manor any more than Prissy had returned to Denbridge village.

He knew only one thing for certain, and it made his heart heavy. Either she had lied to him altogether, or else she had told the truth but made very sure that he would never find her. Either way, there was nothing at all to give him comfort. Either way Priss had very deliberately put a complete end to their liaison with no intention of ever being persuaded to come back again.

He should leave it at that, he decided in the last stages of his journey. If she was unhappy, then that was the way she had wished it. She had made her own decision. He had no more responsibility toward her. He was free of her.

But of course, he discovered after he had returned, even if his conscience was free, his heart was not. He called on Miss Blythe again.

"Did you send me deliberately on a wild-goose chase?" he asked her.

She raised her eyebrows. "A wild-goose chase, sir?" she asked. "You did not discover anything about Prissy? I thought you would."

"Then she must have deceived you about her whereabouts," he said.

"Ah," she said, "but I did not ever expect that you would find her in person, Sir Gerald."

He looked at her and frowned. And swallowed.

"Miss Priscilla Wentworth?" he said, his voice almost a whisper. "She cannot be Priss. Can she?"

"Did you not ever feel that your mistress

was out of the ordinary way?" she asked him.

He merely stared at her. "A lady?" he said. "But why?"

"For the same reason as a girl from the gutter," she said. "From a desire to live a little longer in this wonderful world, Sir Gerald. Her father died, leaving her to the care of her brother. They were an extraordinarily close and loving family. Unfortunately her brother died only days after his father, and in the way of young men, he did not have a will. Everything passed to the next heir."

"Mr. Oswald Wentworth," Sir Gerald said.

"He and his wife made her life hell," Miss Blythe said. "She came to London to teach at my finishing school. I had been her governess for eight years. Unfortunately, she did not understand until after she left home and had been told that she could never expect to return what type of finishing school it is that I run. She was too proud to accept any of the jobs I would have invented for her. She insisted on working for an honest living. She meant the word 'honest' quite literally."

"God," he said, closing his eyes. "Where is she?"

"Safe," she said. "And far more contented

than I hoped for even in the deepest recesses of my heart. She has found people who have accepted her once again as Miss Priscilla Wentworth."

"There was no marriage pending, then," he said.

"No."

"She just wanted to be away from me," he said. "She let me down as gently as she could. I might have expected it of Priss."

She said nothing.

He squared his shoulders and looked up at her. "Thank you, ma'am," he said. "I am glad I know. I will not take any more of your time."

"Why not come back this evening, Sir Gerald?" she asked. "Sonia has one free hour and Margaret, too. Have you had Margaret? She has something of a regular following."

"Thank you," he said. "But no. Good day to you, ma'am."

She looked after him long after the door had closed behind him, a frown on her face, her eyes troubled.

He was glad after all, Sir Gerald thought, that he had agreed to spend at least part of the summer at Severn Park. He could not bear the thought of going down to

Brookhurst, though he supposed that he must spend at least a week or two there so that he could visit all his tenants in person and listen to all the suggestions or grievances that they would inevitably have.

Severn Park was a property he was eager to see, since it was reputed to include one of the great houses and parks of England. The earl had not resided there before, preferring to live in his own boyhood home during the period of his mourning.

And Sir Gerald was glad to be there because there was congenial company and no pressure on him to do or be anything he did not wish to do or be. It was true that, at first, the countess went out of her way to invite neighbors who had young daughters and to seat him beside them at meals or in carriages. But that stopped after her husband had a word with her in Sir Gerald's hearing.

"Gerald is absolutely not interested in having either a wife or a flirt found for him, Abby," he said to her. "Are you, Ger?"

Sir Gerald laughed. "Actually, no, ma'am," he said, "though I do appreciate the goodness of your heart that makes you wish to see to my happiness. I am quite perfectly happy in the single state."

"No, you are not," she said with the frankness that sometimes set him back on his heels. "You are pining for a lost love. Miles has told me so. But I will not harass you any longer. If you choose to be unhappy, then Miles and I will make you as comfortable as we may."

She was, he was glad to find over the coming weeks, as good as her word.

Of course, the countess had a great deal to occupy her mind quite apart from his happiness. Miss Seymour was indeed at Severn Park, but then so was Mr. Boris Gardiner, the countess's brother. And there was a betrothal between them to be celebrated early in the summer and a wedding to be planned for the early autumn before Mr. Gardiner purchased his commission in the Guards and bore off his new bride to follow him and the drum.

The countess was in her element. She also had her two young half-sisters to fuss over, having been restored to them when her marriage released her from poverty and the necessity of earning her own living.

And if all that were not enough, there was the fact that she was preparing to bear Miles's child very early in the new year. His friend had wasted no time, Sir Gerald thought, doing some mental calculations. Lady Severn showed no embarrassment over her condition but talked about it frequently and with some eagerness.

Everything about the Countess of Severn was eager. And Miles was in love with her. And she with him. Despite the hasty and inauspicious beginning to their marriage, they were happy together. Life had good fortune to hand out to some people, Sir Gerald thought with something of a sigh. He was just one of the less fortunate ones.

Not that there was any great surprise in his own fate. It was what he had learned to expect of life. For years he had told himself that he would never again get himself involved in any sort of relationship with a woman. It was the reason he had never married. It was the reason he had been wary about taking a mistress. But he had taken one and he had kept her too long and he had developed an attachment to her. And she had, of course, rejected him.

It was the pattern of his life. He was not going to rage against it. It was his own fault that he had allowed Priss to move into a position from which she could hurt him. He did not blame her. She had been as kind as she could. If he had not foolishly gone looking for her, he would have never known that she had left him for no other reason than to be away from him.

He was intending to spend two more weeks at Severn before taking himself reluctantly off to Brookhurst at the end of August, one week after the wedding of Boris Gardiner and Laura Seymour. The weather was not nearly as good as it had been the previous summer, with the result that they took every opportunity that presented itself to be out-of-doors.

One afternoon, all seven of them went for a lengthy walk, despite the fact that the wind buffeted them as soon as they were away from the shelter of the house. The little girls ran on ahead, the earl, his lady, and Sir Gerald following, and the betrothed pair brought up the rear.

"You will be driving yourself insane over the wedding plans, Abby," the earl said, drawing her hand through his arm and patting it. "Time to blow away the cobwebs."

"And bonnets and ribbons and hairpins, too," she said. "And I have the strange feeling that my words are being blown straight back down my throat so that everyone will think me mute. That would be a dreadful thing. I imagine you would be in a panic and sending for the physician without delay."

"A mute Abby would have to be a sick Abby," her brother agreed. "But we hear you loud and clear back here, don't we, Laura?"

Lady Severn laughed.

The earl looked down at her and frowned in mock dismay. "Abby," he said. "Too many cream cakes, my love. And too many sweets. I am going to have to instruct Cook to starve you for a week."

The wind, blowing the flimsy muslin of her dress against her, had revealed the slight rounding of her figure.

She laughed merrily. "Starve me if you wish, my dear lord," she said, "but I know you will not have the heart to starve your heir or your daughter, whichever this happens to be. I feel quite safe."

"We will be embarrassing you, Ger," the earl said with a chuckle, "talking so openly on such an indelicate subject. Change it, Abby. Tell us about something else."

"The wedding," she said brightly while her husband groaned.

Too many cream cakes.

The blood hammered against Sir Gerald's temples. His heart pounded against his ribs. He was having difficulty drawing breath, setting one foot ahead of the other, remembering where he was.

Too many cream cakes. Priss naked in bed, her back against him, his arms about her, his hand spread over her stomach. Her rounded stomach.

Too many cream cakes. Or perhaps it is the jam tarts. I am going to have to talk to Mrs. Wilson and get her to starve you for a few weeks.

And Priss, almost immediately after, telling him about her letter and her offer of marriage. And leaving him in a hurry within the following few days.

Priss's rounded stomach. Her rounded womb.

The earl and countess were both laughing, something they did frequently.

"Don't you think so, Sir Gerald?" the countess asked him.

"Don't you dare humor her if you know what is good for you, Ger," the earl said.

"What?" he asked, dazed. "I'm sorry. Look, Miles, I have to go back. I have to go. I . . . Excuse me." He turned and hurried away, back in the direction of the house, passing clumsily between the betrothed couple as he did so.

The earl appeared at his side as he hurried along.

"Ger?" he said. "Is something wrong?"

"No, nothing," Sir Gerald said. "I have to go, that's all."

"To the house?" the earl asked. "Or away

from Severn Park?"

"I have to go," Sir Gerald said.

"That's what I thought," Lord Severn said. "What was said or done, Ger? Our talking about Abby's pregnancy would not so discompose you, would it?"

Sir Gerald stopped walking abruptly and turned to face his friend. "How many months with child is she?" he asked.

The earl frowned his incomprehension. "Close to four," he said. "I should not have said what I did about its beginning to show, Ger. I am sorry. It is just that Abby and I are quite ridiculously pleased with ourselves, as if we are the only couple ever to have been so clever."

"Four months," Sir Gerald said, staring blankly at the earl. "April." He lifted one hand and counted off his fingers. "Five more. May, June, July, August, September. Sometime in September. And this is the second half of August."

"Ger." The earl clasped his hands behind his back and looked closely at his friend. "What the devil are you talking about?"

"She may have only a month left," Sir Gerald said. "Perhaps less. I have to go, Miles."

"Ger!" Lord Severn looked at him in exasperation. "Would a fist to the nose do any good?"

"I made the exact same crack about cream cakes," Sir Gerald said. "In April, Miles. She was gone a few days later. I thought it was because she did not want me. I thought she made up that story so that I would not be hurt."

"Prissy?"

"Perhaps it was not so," Sir Gerald said. "Perhaps it was not that at all, Miles. Perhaps she thought I would reject her when I knew. Perhaps she thought I would not want to have anything to do with her or — or . . ."

"Your child," the earl said.

"Perhaps she did not want to go at all." Sir Gerald turned and began to walk again. "And even if she did, Miles. Even if she did. What is she going through now? All alone. I have to go."

"Yes," Lord Severn said, falling into step beside him again. "I can see that you do. And I never did quite believe that she tired of you, Ger. Not Prissy. She was too fond of you. Are you sure about the other, though? A chance remark that both you and I made . . ."

"I am sure," Sir Gerald said. "I may have a very strong tendency to blindness, Miles, but when I finally see, I am almost blinded again by the light."

"Well, then," the Earl of Severn said. "We will have to get you packed and ready to go as soon as we possibly can. Or sooner."

"You will find her at Fairlight in Sussex," Miss Blythe said at long last. "It is a small village on the coast."

Sir Gerald blew his breath out from puffed cheeks. He had almost despaired of getting the information out of her.

"Thank you," he said.

"Sir Gerald," she said, looking steadily and severely at him, "I have done something that I have never done before and never thought to do. And I am not at all sure that I have done the right thing. She is contented where she is. Almost all of the villagers are elderly and rather lonely people, I gather. They have welcomed her with open arms although the foolish girl rejected my advice and was honest with them about herself from the start."

"And you are afraid that I will disturb her contentment?" he asked.

"I know you will disturb her contentment," she said, "but will it be for her greater happiness? That is the question that will give me sleepless nights."

Sir Gerald stared at the floor between

them for a while, deep in thought. "Perhaps she needs to be honest with me, too," he said. "Perhaps when she has been, she will be able to choose the contentment she wants and live with it for the rest of her life. Perhaps she needs to see me one more time."

"She is like the daughter I never had," Miss Blythe said rather sadly.

He lifted his eyes to hers. "She is like the wife I have never yet had, ma'am," he said. "I suppose the fact should make us allies, not enemies."

She smiled very slightly. "Perhaps I will have to modify a certain talk I sometimes have to deliver to some of my girls," she said. "Perhaps hope is never quite dead, even for the most downtrodden and despised members of the human race."

"Or for the more privileged," he said softly.

17

She had not gone down to the beach many times in the past month or so. Though the path was not dangerously steep, it was difficult to keep her balance on the way down, and the weight of her pregnancy made the climb back up an arduous one.

But today she had gone down, drawn by the sparkle of the sun off the waves of the sea and by the sunlight on the sand. The sky was deep blue, the sea a shade deeper again. It was a perfect day in an imperfect summer.

But it had not by any means been a dreary summer. As she tackled the climb back to her cottage, telling herself that there was no hurry, that she might take all of half an hour if she pleased, Priscilla counted her blessings. And they were many.

There were some younger people and families on the farms surrounding the village, but in Fairlight itself almost all the inhabitants were older people, living either alone or in couples. They had taken her into their hearts and had made her excitement at the approaching birth their excitement. They were forever plying her with words of advice, frequently conflicting. There was Mrs. Whiting, for example, who would have her sit all day long with her feet elevated, if she had her way. And there was Miss Cork, who recommended a brisk walk along the beach every morning and evening.

Mr. and Mrs. Jinkerson, who had retired from the pressures of running a business in London seven years before, offered her a job. Mrs. Jinkerson was frequently lonely, her husband explained, and could not get about as she had used to do. Both of them would be more grateful than they could say if Miss Wentworth would keep her company — say for three afternoons a week? They would be pleased to pay her for her time.

Priscilla had assured them that she would be delighted to give Mrs. Jinkerson her company but that she had no wish to be paid.

But they insisted.

"People who have been in business, you see, Miss Wentworth," Mr. Jinkerson had explained to her, "are easier in their mind if they pay for every favor. Then there can be no question of debt."

Priscilla had accepted their goodness, knowing very well that Mrs. Jinkerson was never lonely, but had a whole host of friends in the village. And it had never been noticeable that she found it difficult to get about, either.

Other villagers were beginning to touch upon the idea that they could use this or that help with their daily lives — never anything onerous or ungenteel. Mr. Fibbins, for example, found that his eyesight was failing him at the age of seventy-two and that he needed someone to read his favorite books to him if he was ever to read them again. And, of course, he would be pleased to pay for the favor.

Priscilla paused in her slow upward climb and set a hand below the swelling of her pregnancy in an attempt to ease some of its weight. The sun had moved over to the west. Someone was standing beside the path at the top of the cliff. But the sun was behind him. She could not see who he was. She was in for a scold, she thought with a smile, if it was Vicar Whiting and he bore tales home to his wife.

The villagers took care of their own, the vicar had said during his very first visit to her cottage. He had spoken the simple truth. She had been accepted as one of their own.

She resumed her climb. Her blessings were so many that sometimes in the privacy of her own cottage she wept with the wonder of it. She was being given a second chance.

And if sometimes in the evenings when she was at home behind the drawn curtains of her windows, she felt a loneliness, and a longing for the sound of one particular voice and the sight of one particular face, then she would turn her thoughts to her child, who would be born within the month.

She would not be lonely when her child was born. And perhaps it would be a son. Perhaps he would look like his father. But son or daughter, fair or dark, the child would be half Gerald's. She would find something of him in the child.

Sir Gerald watched her come slowly up the sandy path. Although she had looked up at him, he knew that she had not recognized him. The late afternoon sun was behind him.

He had difficulty catching his breath for a while. She was huge with child.

Despite the slowness of her progress, there was an easiness about her movements, a look of relaxation, as if she had nowhere in particular to go and no time limit in which to get there. She looked happy.

And her face matched the image, he saw when she drew closer. Her eyes were dreamy, her lips drawn up into the suggestion of a smile. She was wearing the straw bonnet he had bought for her the previous year.

Finally, when she was quite close to him, she looked up at him again, shading her eyes.

"Hello, Priss," he said.

She stood quite still for a long time, the sun full on her, making of her a glowing, vital creature, large with the evidence of her fertility. Her expression did not noticeably change.

The strange thing was, she thought, that she was hardly surprised. The final stages of her pregnancy had made her lethargic, dreamy, not quite centered on reality. She thought of him and dreamed of him almost constantly.

She knew he was real, that he really was standing there. But she was hardly surprised.

"Hello, Gerald," she said. And she walked up the remaining stretch of the path to join him on the clifftop. "I did not believe that she would have told you."

"I don't believe she would have," he said,

"if I had raged or threatened. I think she finally came to realize that if she ever wanted her sitting room to herself again, she must tell me where you were."

He was not wearing a hat. The sun was playing with his hair, making of it a fair halo. He looked so very familiar. Oh, so very dearly familiar.

"Why?" she asked. "Why did you want to know, Gerald?"

"Priss," he said. "You should have told me. Why did you not tell me?"

He had always thought her pretty. He thought her beautiful now. That was his child, he thought, looking down at her great bulk, which was arching her back slightly. His. And hers. It was their child.

"I had broken the rules," she said, "and committed the cardinal sin of whores. I allowed myself to be got with child."

"Priss," he said, "you were not a whore. You were my mistress. My woman. I cared for you. Did you not know that?"

It had all been clear in his mind during his journey from London. He had pictured the scene, rehearsed the words, imagined her broken and bewildered. The Priss who had always met him with a warm smile and outstretched hands and a spring in her step would now be the one needing to be taken up into outstretched arms. He would be the strong one, the one in command of the situation.

She was smiling at him with that new smile, the dreamy one that came straight from her impending motherhood.

"Yes, Gerald, I did," she said. "I did. And I cared for you, too. But I had broken the rules. I had been careless. I had to take the consequences."

"It is not fair, is it," he said, looking into her eyes, marveling that there was no bitterness there, "how everything is enjoyment for us men, provided we have the money to pay for our pleasures, while it is the woman who must take all the responsibility and bear all the burden of the consequences if she is careless, as you put it. Priss, the child is mine. I put it there. I am as responsible as you."

She was grateful. She did not know why Miss Blythe would have broken all her own rules and sent him to her. But she was grateful. She knew now that this was all she needed to make her contentment complete — Gerald visiting her, acknowledging his paternity of her child, telling her he had been fond of her.

Except that tomorrow there would be pain again when he was gone.

She would not think of tomorrow.

"Will you come to my cottage?" she asked. "I have a kettle always boiling."

"You must sit down, Priss," he said, offering her his arm. "Is it a very heavy burden?"

"Mrs. Murdoch — she is the midwife — says that it will fall soon," she said. "Then I will be able to breathe more easily. Of course, then I will find it more difficult to walk. But it will not be for long. Once it has fallen, it will be almost ready for the birth."

"Priss." He set one hand over hers. "When?"

"Two, maybe three weeks," she said. "Did Miss Blythe warn you that this is what you would find?"

"I knew," he said. "You must have thought me an incredible simpleton, Priss. Too many cream cakes, indeed. If Miles had not said the exact same thing to the countess just a week ago, I might never have opened up my eyes."

She preceded him into the cottage and bent over the fire, where the kettle was singing merrily. "The countess is increasing?" she said. "Is Lord Severn happy? I am glad for him."

"I came, Priss," he said. "I would have come months ago, as soon as I discovered who you are, but the only reason I could think of then for your having lied to me was that you had grown tired of me after all and wanted to leave. So I let you go."

She looked up from her task of pouring boiling water into the teapot. "Oh, no, Gerald," she said. "You knew that was not the reason. I told you it was not."

"But what was I to think, Priss?" he asked.

Her hands paused suddenly on the tea cozy as she fitted it over the teapot. She looked up at him.

"After you discovered what?" she said.

"I went down to Denbridge," he said. "It was just after you left, Priss. I wanted to make sure that you were settled happily. I was going to take you back if you weren't, offer you a higher salary, maybe. Kit told me where to go. I didn't realize until after I had left there that the Miss Priscilla Wentworth I had heard mentioned was you. But I put two and two together in my usual tortoiselike way. Why did you not ever tell me, Priss?"

"Downstairs I was your mistress, Gerald," she said. "Upstairs I was myself, someone different. It seemed important to me to keep my two identities separate."

"And you could never share your real self with me?" he asked. "I thought we were friends, Priss. I thought you knew I was fond of you."

"I was your mistress, Gerald," she said. "You paid me to lie with you."

He sat down and set a hand over his eyes. "But it was more than that," he said. "It was, wasn't it? Wasn't it more than that, Priss? To me it was."

She set a cup of tea on the table beside him and sat awkwardly opposite him.

"Thank you for coming," she said. "I am glad you have come. I have thought of you a great deal in the past few weeks."

"There is a clergyman here?" he asked. "I saw the church. Will he marry us tomorrow, do you think, Priss? I don't want to wait any longer. I don't want the child to be born out of wedlock."

He knew he had said the wrong thing. For the first time her expression changed. Devil take it, he thought, but he was so gauche. No formal proposal? No going down on one knee and all that stuff that women set such store by? He ran a hand through his curls.

"There will be no marriage, Gerald," she said. "Is that why you have come? It is good of you. Yes, it is good of you. But please. Let us talk of something else. Tell me more about Lord Severn and his bride."

"Priss," he said, "you are a lady. You are Miss Wentworth of Denton Manor."

No. She did not want this. She did not want this memory of him.

"I am the woman you met at Miss Blythe's, Gerald," she said. "The woman you employed as a mistress for almost a year. I am not suddenly different just because you now know that once upon a time I was Miss Wentworth of Denton. I was not marriageable when I was just Prissy. There is no difference now."

"But there is, Priss," he said. "I know I should have realized it. The evidence was staring me in the face. But I did not. I never suspected that you were a lady."

She got up awkwardly to set the kettle over the fire again. "I am not a lady, Gerald," she said. "Neither am I a whore. I was both but am neither. I am Priscilla Wentworth, resident of Fairlight, supporting myself partly on earnings that I saved and a generous settlement from my former employer and partly on light employment I have been given in the village here. That is all. No labels. Just Priscilla Wentworth. You need not marry me, Gerald, just because you think you must make a lady respectable. You would not have dreamed of marrying me if I had come from the gutter, as you have always supposed."

"Priss." He was on his feet too, hovering

behind her. "That is not the reason. Have I given you the impression that it is? I suppose I have. I am so clumsy with words. There is the child. It's my child. Ours. I have to give you the protection of my name. I must . . ."

She turned to smile at him, her anger of a moment before fading again. "No," she said. "No, Gerald. It is good of you. There are not many men, I believe, who would feel responsible for a child begotten in such a way or for the child's mother. But it is not a good enough reason. And I really do not need the protection of your name. I can scarcely believe it is true myself, but I have been accepted here. I even feel loved here. Here I will not be a fallen woman or my child a bastard. I cannot marry you, Gerald. I would always be burdened by the knowledge that you had married me because of who I am and because you had got me with child. And you would always be burdened by the knowledge that you had been forced into something that you had never wanted in your life."

After all, she did not want him. He had hoped. He had done more than hope. He had dreamed — ever since his realization of the truth at Severn Park a week before. Even more so since his visit to Kit's. He had dreamed throughout his journey from London, picturing it all, the way it would be, himself the hero of the dream.

He drew a package from an inner pocket of his coat and handed it to her.

"It took me almost a week to get this," he said. "It is not an easy thing to do. But I did it. I thought at last I would be able to use it."

She looked down at the special license he had put in her hands. He was that serious, then. The idea of marrying her had not been a spur-of-the-moment thing. He had spent a week getting a special license. The words on the paper blurred before her eyes for a moment.

"Gerald." She handed it back to him. "Thank you, dear. You have always been very good to me. But I will not burden your life with a wife you have never intended to take. Come and visit our child if you wish — as often as you like. I hope you do. But we must not marry. I know you were fond of me. I would prefer to keep that, to be able to think that you will remain fond of me. Perhaps you can do something for our child when he is older — send him to school, perhaps. Or her."

"Priss." He stared at the license before taking it back and returning it to his pocket.

"I want to marry you. I asked you because I want it."

She shook her head.

"Well, then," he said. "There is no more to say, is there? I'll go back to London tomorrow. I'll return when the baby is born. You will let me know?"

"Yes," she said.

He turned without another word, stumbling against the chair he had been sitting on earlier, and found his way to the door. He was outside, with the door closed behind him, before the tears came. He strode off to the cliffs rather than walk back along the street to the inn where he had put up and risk having to pass someone.

And Priscilla, inside the cottage, sat back down on her chair, her hands resting on the swelling beneath her bosom, staring at the kettle, which was humming on the fire again. Two cups of tea grew cold on the table at her elbow.

Fool, she told herself. Fool.

Heaven had been within her grasp and she had rejected it. All of her most impossible dreams could have come true. She could have been married the very next day. To Gerald.

And she had sent him away. Because he had asked for the wrong reasons. Noble reasons, perhaps. But the wrong ones.

Fool. Fool. Fool.

And just a short while ago she had been so happy to see him. He had seemed to be a part of the contentment that her life in the village and her advanced pregnancy had brought her. But a little more than the contentment, too. He had been the missing something that held contentment back from being perfect happiness.

Her lover had come to her again and she had been completely happy. She had not expected permanence, only a brief visit. But then she had never expected permanence with Gerald. She would have been contented with a few hours or perhaps even a few days of happiness. She could have returned to her contentment afterward.

Yet, now she felt bereft. Empty, as she had felt the day she left him. Raw with the pain of loneliness and loss.

The light of late afternoon turned to dusk in the room. But she continued to sit and stare into the dying fire.

The lamp had been lit, the fire built again, the teacups cleared away and washed together with the dinner dishes. Priscilla had forced herself to eat. She sat down finally with her favorite book and read the sonnet he had studied at school.

" 'Shall I compare thee to a summer's day?' " she read. " 'Thou art more lovely and more temperate.' "

There was a knock on the door.

Who? she thought as she got slowly to her feet. Gerald? But she did not want him to come back. It had taken her a few hours to pull herself free of the dreadful lethargy that had kept her sitting in a darkened room and staring into glowing ashes. Please let it be someone else, she prayed silently as she pulled back the bolt and opened the door.

"Priss?" he said. His face looked haunted.

She found herself doing what she had always done when he came to her. She held out her hands for his.

"Gerald," she said. "Come in."

"I just thought of something," he said, coming inside and releasing her hands to close the door. "I was sitting in my room at the inn when it struck me. I should have thought of it sooner. I never could think fast, could I?"

"Gerald," she said. He was gazing at her with eager, anxious eyes. She reached up without thinking to cup one of his cheeks in her hand.

He covered her hand with his. "It was because you weren't convinced, wasn't it?"

he said. "You thought it was just because I knew who you were and because of the baby. You did not quite believe it was because I love you, did you?"

"You did not mention love, Gerald," she said. She brushed at the lapel of his coat with her free hand.

"I did," he said frowning. "I did, Priss. It is the only reason. I must have said it."

She shook her head.

"I can't live without you," he said. "I don't know how, Priss. I keep thinking to tell you something or ask you something. Or I keep thinking to come to you with some problem or with a headache or a cold or something. And then I remember that you are not there. Or I walk past the park or the British Museum and miss you until it hurts. I can't sleep properly at night. And I keep thinking of how you always used to be there last summer when I was awake and kept me company and put me back to sleep again. And when I am sleeping, I wake and reach out for you. And you are not there."

"Gerald," she said, lifting her hand from his lapel to cup his other cheek.

"I came to trust you," he said. "I never thought to trust again after my mother and after Helena. I never told you about Helena, did I? My stepmother? I'll tell you someday.

I trusted you, Priss, because you were always good to me and never demanding and always so sweet and even-tempered. When you lied to me and disappeared and I thought it was because you had not liked to tell me that you had grown tired of me, I wanted to die. I didn't, of course, and I went about my daily business and then went down to Severn with Miles and the countess. But all the time there was the feeling in me that I would prefer to die if only it could be arranged."

She bit her upper lip.

"You aren't crying, are you, Priss?" he said, brushing a curl back from her face, blotting a tear from her lower lashes. "It makes a pathetic story, doesn't it? I didn't mean to put it quite like this. What I meant to say was that perhaps this afternoon you did not realize fully that this was the reason. That you are the only thing in my life that makes me want to live it, Priss. Like some priceless little jewel in the middle of a desert. Or something like that. I never was good with words."

"No," she said, swallowing to take the high pitch from her voice. "I didn't realize what you meant this afternoon, Gerald."

"I thought you didn't," he said. "And then it struck me, Priss."

"What did?" she asked.

"You didn't read the license, did you?" he said. "I mean, you saw it was a special license, and you gave it back to me because you didn't want to use it. But you didn't read it, did you?"

She shook her head.

"Read it," he said, reaching into his pocket while she dropped her hands away from his face. "Look at the date, Priss. The date it was issued."

She looked down at the paper and followed the direction of his pointing finger.

"April," she said.

"You can check it with Kit if you like," he said. "It was before I went to Wiltshire, Priss. I took it with me just in case you decided you would settle for me instead of that swain who wanted you back. I thought that perhaps, after seeing him again, you would realize that you were no longer fond of him. I thought perhaps you would take me instead."

She bit her lip again for a moment. "You said this afternoon that you were going to offer me a higher salary," she said.

"If you did not want to marry me," he said. "If perhaps you wanted to take me on only for another year or perhaps two or until you really did grow tired of me."

"Gerald," she said.

"And you can see that I had the license long before I knew about the child," he said. "I got it for only one reason, Priss. You must see that now."

"Yes," she said, handing it back to him. "Yes."

"Come back to me," he said. "Please, Priss. Marry me. Or if you don't want anything so permanent, well, come back to me anyway. And when you want to leave, I will provide for you and the child. I know I'm not much, but I will look after you. If only things had been different, I know you could have done so much better for yourself. You are so intelligent and knowledgeable and accomplished. I know I have nothing much to offer someone like you, but . . ."

"Gerald!" she said, and her hands were rubbing hard against the lapels of his coat. "You have everything to offer me. Everything in the world. In the whole universe. Your love. A loyal and a warm and kind heart. Yourself. You are so very worthy of being loved, and all I can offer you is a soiled life."

He covered her hands with his and held them flat against his chest. He was shaking his head. "You survived, Priss," he said. "You worked for your living. And I am glad you did or I would never have met you. It is in the past, those months at Kit's. In the past, where it will stay."

"You are a baronet," she said. "I will never be accepted, Gerald. Never received."

"I think you are wrong," he said. "There are perfectly respectable people in society who have a far more scarlet past than yours. But even if you are right, it does not matter. It's you I want, Priss. Only you. We will live it through together, whatever may be facing us. And I know Miles will receive you, and the countess, too. She hugged me when I was leaving and even kissed my cheek. I was never so surprised in my life."

"Gerald." She looked at him with troubled eyes. "Are you sure? Are you very sure?"

He smiled at her suddenly, more radiantly than she had ever seen him smile before.

"You are going to say yes, aren't you?" he said. "I know that you are. Say it, Priss. I want to hear it. I have dreamed of this moment for months and never believed that it would really come. Say it. Will you marry me?"

She leaned her head forward and rested her forehead between her hands against his chest.

"Yes," she said.

"Tonight," he said. "I called on the vicar

before I came here, Priss, and asked him. We can go tonight. You are going to be my wife before another hour has passed."

"I thought you did not believe that I would say yes," she said.

"I didn't," he said. "But a fellow can dream. It was a good part of the dream, talking to the vicar and watching his wife throw her apron over her head and burst into tears. I think they must be fond of you, Priss."

"Gerald," she said, lifting her head and patting one hand against his heart. "Tonight. Tonight? Now?"

"There is one thing I want to do first, though," he said. "May I, Priss? One thing I long to do."

He took her by the shoulders, turned her, and drew her back against him. And he put his arms about her and spread his hands over her, moving them slowly, feeling the new contours of her body, the enlarged firm breasts, the swelling beneath.

"Is it heavy, Priss?" he asked. "The child is heavy?"

"Yes," she said. "And active. Always kicking and punching me."

"I wish I had been with you the whole time," he said wistfully, setting his cheek against her curls as she rested her head back on his shoulder. “I wish I could have watched and felt it grow along with you, Priss, our child.”

“I have told it about its father every single day,” she said.

“Have you?” He turned his head and kissed her. “Priss, I do love you. It was not a ruse to get you to say yes.”

“I know,” she said. “I know that, Gerald. I loved you even before I left Miss Blythe’s, you know. You were always very special to me, right from the first moment I saw you.”

“I don’t know why,” he said. “There is nothing at all special about me, Priss.”

“Then we have a quarrel,” she said, turning her head so that their mouths could meet more comfortably. She smiled warmly into his eyes. “And I shall spend the rest of my life proving that I am right, Gerald. I can be a dreadfully stubborn opponent. I never lose an argument. And I say you are very, very special.”

He kissed her.

“I can’t even turn you around to do this more thoroughly, can I?” he said. “It’s not triplets by any chance, is it, Priss?”

“No,” she said, turning anyway in his arms and watching him look down in wonder and delight at the bulk that came between them. “Just a few too many cream cakes, Gerald.

And jam tarts, of course. I never could resist a jam tart."

He set his arms gently about her, afraid of hurting her, afraid of squashing their baby, and kissed her.

And it was a very good thing, too, he told her several hours later when he lay behind her in her bed at the cottage, supporting her aching back against his own body, his arms about her, one hand spread again over her bulk — it was a very good thing she said yes. By the time they arrived at the church, it had been half filled with smiling, nodding villagers — almost all of them elderly.

"A very good thing, Priss," he said, rubbing his cheek against her curls. "I have the strong feeling that they would all have been severely disappointed if you had said no."

"I am glad you told them all that we would stay here for the birth of the baby, Gerald," she said. "The baby belongs to this village almost as much as to us."

"We will bring him down on his birthday every year," he said. "And maybe once or twice more each year, too. Time to sleep now, Priss. You must need plenty of rest."

"Yes," she said with a sigh of contentment, turning her head to kiss his arm beneath it. "Gerald, I am so very, very happy."

"Are you?" he said. "Are you really, Priss? I still can't quite believe what a lucky devil I am."

She sighed again.

"Good night, Lady Stapleton," he said.

"Oh," she said. "Yes, I am, aren't I? How strange and how lovely it sounds. Lady Stapleton! Good night, Gerald."

The employees of Thorndike Press hope you have enjoyed this Large Print book. All our Thorndike, Wheeler, and Kennebec Large Print titles are designed for easy reading, and all our books are made to last. Other Thorndike Press Large Print books are available at your library, through selected bookstores, or directly from us.

For information about titles, please call:
(800) 223-1244

or visit our Web site at:
http://gale.cengage.com/thorndike

To share your comments, please write:
Publisher
Thorndike Press
295 Kennedy Memorial Drive
Waterville, ME 04901